"Don't you ever get lonely, Rebecca?"

Slade asked the question in a soft insidious drawl that wound around her brittle defences.

"Perhaps that's why I want a child."

"Exactly." He walked toward her, his eyes holding hers in challenge. "Doesn't it seem wasteful to turn me away when I'm right here on your doorstep? On your own admission, you find me attractive enough to consider having a child by me. So why not take this opportunity, Rebecca? Why not go for what you want?"

She could not wrench her eyes from the hypnotic challenge in his. She could feel her heart hammering wildly. Her mouth had gone completely dry. She knew she should somehow deny all he said, but she could not find the will to take that critical step away from him.

"You can tell me to go...or ask me to stay. Make your choice, Rebecca."

EMMA DARCY nearly became an actress until her fiancé declared he preferred to attend the theater *with* her. She became a wife and mother. Later, she took up oil painting—unsuccessfully, she remarks. Then she tried architecture, designing the family home in New South Wales. Next came romance writing—"the hardest and most challenging of all the activities," she confesses.

Books by Emma Darcy

Don't miss any of our special offers. Write to us at the following address for information on our newest releases.

Harlequin Reader Service
P.O. Box 1397, Buffalo, NY 14240
Canadian address: P.O. Box 603,
Fort Erie, Ont. L2A 5X3

EMMA DARCY

to tame a wild heart

Harlequin Books

TORONTO • NEW YORK • LONDON
AMSTERDAM • PARIS • SYDNEY • HAMBURG
STOCKHOLM • ATHENS • TOKYO • MILAN
MADRID • WARSAW • BUDAPEST • AUCKLAND

For Karin,
a lovely, loving person
who can make the impossible happen

Harlequin Presents first edition May 1992
ISBN 0-373-11455-9

TO TAME A WILD HEART

CHAPTER ONE

SLADE CORDELL SHIFTED restlessly in the high-backed leather chair that had belonged to his father before him. It *was* uncomfortable, damned uncomfortable. Like a lot of things in this boardroom, he decided.

The thought was part of a chain of discontented thoughts that had passed through his mind since the beginning of this particular meeting. Just lately—no, it was more than just lately—for longer than he cared to remember, all his responsibilities concerning Cordell Enterprises had begun to pall on him.

His eyes flicked around the men seated on either side of the long mahogany table. They were all top executives. Otherwise they wouldn't be holding the positions they did. Slade wondered if he was really necessary or nothing more than a figurehead. Could he let the reins slide, or would everything start to fall apart if he wasn't there to hold it together in a cohesive working pattern? It was an interesting thought.

Cordell Enterprises was a vast octopus organisation. The oil fields in Texas had started it, together with a small minority holding in a company that made bits for mining drills. That had been the foundation of the Howard Hughes fortune. Cordell Enterprises had shared in it, albeit to a much smaller degree. Now the octopus had tentacles that stretched halfway around the world, embracing such diverse interests as electronics and pharmaceuticals and beef cattle. The

American corporate offices took up six floors of the modern office block on Park Avenue, right in the heart of New York, but this was only the nerve centre. There were other offices: Dallas, London, Paris...

For more than ten years Slade had kept tabs on the rapidly shifting inner worlds of international business, sometimes stealing a step on them, never falling behind. He didn't like losing—never had—yet the spice of winning simply wasn't there any more. He was tired—tired of thinking, tired of travelling, tired of listening to reports on which he was always expected to pass judgement, tired and bored!

Maybe he just needed a long vacation to get rid of this burnt-out feeling. Yet a man could hardly be burnt out at thirty-six. He had too many years ahead of him to allow that as a reality. He simply needed something to liven up this dog-day existence. An adventure. A new sense of purpose. But what?

He dragged his concentration together and listened to the end of the report being given on future oil contracts and prices. Nothing to worry about there. Hinkman was one of the best directors on the board, comprehensive in his diligence, even when the incomprehensible happened, which it did from time to time.

The door to the boardroom burst open.

Slade's attention was galvanised. Board meetings were secret, privileged and inviolable!

A woman in red whirled into the room, hurling a defiant message over her shoulder. "If this is a full board meeting, I couldn't have chosen a better time!"

She swung on her heel and strode purposefully to the foot of the table where she came to a halt. Her eyes blazed straight down the length of it to where Slade sat in the high backed leather chair, which designated his status. Her chin tilted in resolute pride and self-determination.

"Mr. Slade Cordell..." Her fist made a belligerent ball and pressed down on the table in an emphatic gesture of intent. "I've come to add one more item to the agenda of this meeting. As a matter of urgency, sir!"

The "sir" held a trace of contempt that piqued his curiosity. The accent was unmistakably Australian, which piqued his curiosity even more. Skin bronzed, athletic build, loose limbed. She looked like she could go anywhere, do anything... and get her own way. Slade felt a very real stirring of interest. She was also quite strikingly attractive.

There had been a surfeit of beautiful women in Slade's life, and beauty alone was no longer a drawing card to him. They had to have more than that—an individuality, a charm. But even those words seemed lukewarm for this woman. There was an aura of boldness about her, a fiery steel that nothing had ever tempered.

A couple of the board members started to rise, preparing to eject her. Slade made a motion with his hand to stop them. Ron Colson, the secretary who was supposed to ensure there were no interruptions, made an agitated appearance in the doorway.

"I beg your pardon, sir. She went straight past me without a—"

Slade flicked a look at the flustered secretary, silencing the man without a word. In the usual course of events he would not tolerate such a breach of privacy. Later on the secretary would certainly get the broadside he deserved. Apart from anything else, it kept the staff on its toes. More importantly, it ensured that in future he anticipated what had never happened before! That, surely, was his job!

However, Slade was not displeased with this particular diversion. In a perverse kind of way he welcomed something wild happening, especially when it wasn't supposed to. He rose to his feet to get a better look at the situation.

The young woman's chin tilted higher as she took in his full height. His six-foot-four-inch frame was amply filled. Slade had played football in college, and the physique developed then was in no way diminished. He was well aware that most people found him formidable, and not only because he headed Cordell Enterprises. But this woman wasn't intimidated. Not in any shape or form. She glared at him as though he was nothing but a big ape who needed to be put in his place.

"How do you do, ma'am?" he said in his most exaggerated Texas drawl, then gave her a smile designed to wipe out all hostility within its radius. "You got it right. I surely am Slade Cordell."

The look of surprise on her face was worth this bit of acting. She hadn't expected that. She had erupted into the room, all steamed up for a fight and determined to win. Well, she wasn't going to get a fight.

He glanced around the table. Everyone was tensely waiting for his true reaction, not believing for one moment that this good humour was genuine. One or two tried a smile just in case it was what he wanted.

Yes-men! Maybe that was the source of his problem. He needed someone who could stand up to him, someone with balls, someone without fear who had the courage of his convictions, someone like this woman who was emanating the kind of boldness that refused to recognise backward steps.

Not even Hinkman did that. They were all good executives, but only managers. Slade saw that more clearly now. They had reached the top rung of their abilities. He *was* necessary, the linchpin that set them all in motion.

Well, he would make certain he was right about that.

He turned an affable face towards the secretary, who was too frightened to believe in it. "Mr Colson, would you be kind enough to bring this young lady a chair so that she can sit in and help this board with its deliberations?"

That should create a volcanic explosion, Slade thought. One or more of these board members should erupt like Krakatoa did, back in 1883. The world should move!

Dead silence.

No eruption.

No one moved.

Not a word of protest was uttered.

All yes-men!

No, not quite all. Ross Harper's eyes met his, a quizzical challenge in them. Harper was the most junior board member. New blood brought in from outside the organisation and still feeling his way. Someone to be watched and encouraged, Slade noted approvingly.

After a few frozen seconds, Colson nervously propelled himself into action. A chair was brought. The lady was seated. Slade waved Colson out. The door closed very quietly behind him. The board members sat around the table, looking down at the papers in front of them. They knew they should have demurred, knew they should have opposed this unbelievably ridiculous idea that an absolute stranger could help them make top-level business decisions. They hadn't. Only Ross Harper had even thought of doing so.

It cleared Slade's mind of a lot of misconceptions. He was most assuredly needed here. Without him, Cordell Enterprises would be an octopus without a head, its tentacles turning in on themselves, all momentum coming to a halt. All these executive positions needed a real shake-up. Fancy letting a young woman get the better of them! It both amused Slade and disgusted him.

He sat back in his chair. It felt more comfortable than it had in a long time. He suddenly felt more alive than he had done in a long time. Sparking on all cylinders! His eyes drifted to the woman in red. In his mind, Slade raised an imaginary hat. *Thank you, ma'am,* he said to himself. *You don't know how much you've already helped me.*

She stared at him, a curious look of reassessment in her eyes. Shrewd and intelligent, he thought. Certainly she hadn't missed some of the nuances of what was going on in this room and she was concentrating solely on him, dismissing all the others as unimportant ciphers. Which was how they had acted. Slade took his time returning her appraisal. It was a deliberate tactic—testing her nerve, reinforcing his authority and noting all the details that revealed information about her.

The linen suit she wore was not precisely red. It was a more subtle shade, coral, perhaps, but all the more distinctive for being slightly unusual. Silk blouse. Nice pieces of jewelry, rather Victorian in style but undoubtedly genuine. A woman of considerable class, he decided, from a family of some wealth. Possibly a lot of wealth.

Slade turned his attention to reading what character he could from her face.

Her glossy black hair was pulled back from a striking widow's peak and wound into a neat coif around her head. The severe hairstyle suggested that vanity came second place to practicality. Nevertheless, it did serve to accentuate the wide brow and prominent cheekbones and draw attention to the fine elegance of a squarish jawline. There was no hint of weakness in those features. Her nose seemed rather thin for such a strong-boned face, but the flare of her nostrils was wide enough to complement the full-lipped mouth.

Passion, he thought. She certainly had passion. It was a thought that stirred another kind of interest. He wondered how passionate she would be...but this was the board-room, not a bedroom. Slade dragged his mind back to business.

She had borne his study of her without the minutest re-action, not even a slight flinch or quiver. Slade knew there were few men who could have withstood such an examina-tion with complete sangfroid. It took a strength of charac-ter, or purpose, that would not be shaken under any duress.

Admiration kindled his interest further as he levelled his gaze on hers—green eyes, thickly lashed and blazing with pride and anger. He had no doubt, however, that the anger was under control. She was merely letting him know that his long silent scrutiny had induced only a measure of scorn from her. There was not the slightest waver in eye contact. A blistering challenge. Rock steady.

Slade found her response intriguing, all the more so since she looked so young. He placed her age in the early twen-ties, but he could be mistaken about that. She had the kind of face that would hold age indefinitely. Whatever her ex-perience of life, she had learned an inner strength that was rare amongst the women he knew. His curiosity deepened.

"I have not had the pleasure of your acquaintance, ma'am," he said, his mouth curling into a smile that was meant to disarm her. "If you would be so kind as to intro-duce yourself..."

She did not smile back. She did not relax one muscle. There was a bitter flash in her eyes as she answered him. "Rebecca Wilder, Mr. Cordell. I am the granddaughter of Janet Wilder."

She spoke those names as though they should have meant something to him, as though she had taken the biggest piece of artillery out of the U.S. arsenal, aimed it between his eyes and pressed the trigger. Yet they meant nothing to him. He mentally processed all the names he knew. None fitted.

"I'm pleased to meet you, ma'am," he said.

The glitter of savage mockery in her eyes told him that she didn't believe him, that she no longer believed her mission could be accomplished, whatever it was. But she had to feel passionately about that mission or she would not have broken into this boardroom to confront him.

"What can we do for you?" he asked softly, every instinct telling him that there was something wrong about this situation. Something badly wrong. And he felt a strong need to make it right, because Rebecca Wilder... Darn it! Was it Miss or Mrs.? He would have to watch her hands for rings.

"I do not like to see cattle suffer, Mr. Cordell. Not even your cattle," she bit out angrily. "My grandmother has done all she can to prevent that from happening up until now. But no more, Mr. Cordell. You either sell off the cattle your land won't support or Devil's Elbow will become their graveyard."

"Devil's Elbow?" A stirring of memory that he couldn't place accurately yet.

Scorn glared back at him. "It was called that long before you bought it, Mr. Cordell. For good reason, if you had ever bothered to find out. However, your new name for it—may God have mercy on your avaricious soul—is Logan's Run."

Facts slotted into place. He had renamed that property in Australia after Grandfather Logan. At the time it had seemed a good idea even though he had never seen the cattle ranch in question. It had just been another acquisition among many.

What had gone wrong? What gross mismanagement was going on behind his back? What was being hidden from him? Maybe it was time he looked beyond executive levels and did some spot checks on the lower echelons of his organisation.

"You're telling me that the cattle on Logan's Run are in danger of dying?" His voice held a cutting edge that had no shade of affability left in it. None at all. His mind was very sharply back on business.

"That's precisely what I'm telling you," she confirmed. "Unless we see some positive action from you within a week—action that will redress the situation you've created—we will take whatever steps are necessary to protect ourselves and others from your blind intransigence. In case you are in any doubt as to the outcome, Mr. Cordell, that means your cattle will start to die. And that's all I have to say to you."

She stood up, her bearing one of haughty contempt as she looked down the table at him. "I've travelled halfway around the world to tell you that, Mr. Cordell. I've spent the last five days trying to reach you to tell you that." Her eyes glittered their scorn for him and his organisation. "I tried the telephone, the telex, the fax and any other machine I could get hold of. I tried..."

Her left hand performed an expressive dismissal. No rings, Slade noted.

"Well, I tried just about everything. And I tried everybody I could find. Without success. But now you've been told, Mr. Cordell. And I know you've been told," she said with grim satisfaction.

Her chin lifted in determined pride. "I've done what I came to do. We've had no co-operation from your people at Devil's Elbow, no co-operation from your people in Brisbane, no co-operation from anyone here at your headquarters in New York. And I expect none from you. But at least now we can make our decisions with a completely clear conscience. You have a week, Mr. Cordell. No more."

Her smile was one of utter disdain. "Have a nice day, Mr. Cordell," she said in mocking mimic of the words that had been tossed so carelessly and meaninglessly at her all week. Then she turned to go.

"Miss Wilder..." He had to stop her. He had to make things right. He wasn't about to let her go on this unsatisfactory note. He didn't want to let her go at all!

She paused. Slade saw the fullness of her lips tighten into a thin line then relax to their natural shape. Very slowly her head turned towards him. One eyebrow was raised in disdainful challenge.

"I'm very grateful to you," Slade said with absolute precision, his words measured like a metronome as he whipped his mind off the personal angle and took the business implications in. "I'd be even more grateful if you would sit down again and clarify this matter, ah, further. It may come as a surprise to you—it comes as a considerably unpleasant surprise to me—" he shot a baleful look around the table "—that I had no knowledge of this situation whatsoever. I aim to remedy that right now. So, please...would you be so kind as to bear with me, and the board, just a little while longer?"

Slade could see she didn't want to. She had no reason to want to. If what she said was true, he was unreasonable to ask it of her. Yet with all the power at his command he willed her to stay, to sit down again, to help him sort out the truth and put everything right between them.

For what seemed a very long time, but was probably only seconds, her eyes bored into his, questioning the integrity of his appeal. Slade savagely regretted his earlier flippancy. It had served one purpose better than he had ever anticipated, but it told against him now. He could feel her weighing everything he had said and done. He didn't know what tipped the balance in her mind, but she sat down again.

The tension eased out of his body.

He had won.

The pleasure, the triumph that rippled through his mind—the tingle of excitement in his belly—stirred Slade to another realisation. He couldn't remember anyone ever challenging him as this woman was; those eyes, glittering green daggers scouring his soul. The urge—the desire—to tame her was the strongest feeling he'd had in a long, long time.

He hadn't won much from her yet, only the most minimal stay of judgement, but he would win a lot more before he was finished with her. Oh, yes, he would!

CHAPTER TWO

FOOL! Rebecca berated herself. She should have walked out. She should have shown Slade Cordell and his men her utter contempt for them and their kind by turning her back on them and walking out without another word. She had finally done what she had set out to achieve, what she had promised Gran she would achieve. The warning had been delivered, right to the top. There was no point in staying.

Yet there had been something compelling in those dark blue eyes, a need, a demand that challenged her to stay, despite all she had been through. A strong man, Slade Cordell. His eyes hadn't once shifted from hers. Not the slightest waver. He had absorbed what she had hurled at him and was demanding more from her.

It was weak and stupid to give in to his wishes now, but no one could ever say of her that she hadn't been absolutely fair. She was bending over backwards to be fair!

"Thank you," he said. As if he really meant it.

Two-faced, she thought furiously. Multi-faced! A face for every situation, switched on and off at will. He wanted to use her. That's why he had asked her to stay. He had been using her from the moment she had stepped into this room, playing some private hand of his own for the purpose of testing his power. Why she had come had been completely irrelevant. Did he think she was so lacking in perception that she couldn't see that?

He leaned forward, resting his forearms on the table. "Now, Miss Wilder," he began.

And that was another thing! How did he know she wasn't married if he truly knew nothing about her? She hadn't told him. He hadn't asked. She looked down at her hands and understood. There should have been rings, if only. . .

"Would you be kind enough to tell me and the board, precisely why my cattle are going to die?"

Rebecca lifted her gaze reluctantly. The dark blue eyes looked keenly interested. Was Slade Cordell a consummate actor? What on earth was being played out here behind the scenes?

Rebecca shrugged off the thought. It wasn't her problem. At least by staying she could get a few shots of her own in. Futile, most likely, but it would ease the heartburn she had suffered over the last few days. However, someone preempted her reply.

"Mr. Cordell."

It was one of the members of the board on the left side of the table. He had leaned forward, his heavy-jowled face turned towards the high-backed leather chair, to the man who occupied that chair with almost chilling dominance.

It was not that Slade Cordell was simply a big man, although he had left no doubt in Rebecca's mind that he used his imposing height and physique to forceful effect. His face was also an asset. It was the kind of face that belonged to a leader, a hard masculine face, uncompromising, authoritative in every line. The wide sweep of his brow was framed by dark hair, almost as dark as her own, thick and straight and cut short with no concession towards the fashion of the day. His nose was sharply ridged but it flared to his cheeks in strong planes. A firm mouth. An even firmer chin. But the power of the man resided in his eyes, those deeply set blue eyes that were now turned coldly to the man who had spoken.

"You have something to say, Mr. Petrie?" The words were drawled from a mouth that curled as it delivered them. The tone was just as soft as before but it now carried a dangerous undercurrent that would make any person think twice before interrupting again.

The man's jowls shook a little as he swallowed.

The blue eyes swung to Rebecca. "Mr. Petrie has the responsibility of reporting to me on our Australian holdings, Miss Wilder. In the normal channeling process of this organisation, you would be passed through him to get to me."

There was a tangible rise of tension around the table. Slade Cordell was certainly a lot younger than Rebecca had expected. He looked to be the youngest man in this room. Nevertheless, there was no doubting who held the whip hand, even in this high-powered company.

"Sir." Mr. Petrie forced a sharp authority into his voice. "If you will simply ask Miss Wilder to wait outside, I'll clear this matter up after the board meeting."

"I have a mind to clear it up myself, Mr. Petrie. I take it you were aware that Miss Wilder was in New York this week...having come all the way from Australia to see me?"

"Yes. But—"

"That she has been shuttled around these offices for days on end?"

"Yes. But—"

"That she was blocked in her purpose no matter what she tried?"

"I was preparing my report for this meeting, sir," Mr. Petrie excused himself.

"Did it occur to you that Miss Wilder might have something to add to your report?" came the softly spoken retort, the dangerous undercurrent even more in evidence.

"May I suggest to you that you look up your report on Logan's Run so that you might have something constructive to add to this discussion?"

Mr. Petrie's face tightened. "I have, sir. I assumed that Miss Wilder's visit here was a negotiating tactic. It seemed the better tactic for us to ignore her request to see you, sir. There is a requisition to our Brisbane branch for the funds to buy the property owned by—"

"We will never sell!" Rebecca hurled at him, infuriated to discover that she had been the victim of tactics on an issue over which there could be no further meaningful discussion. Ever since Pa had died, Cordell Enterprises had been at Gran to sell, as if she ever would! They had been plying their offers for two years now, obdurately intent on changing Gran's mind, never listening to reason, pushing, pushing, pushing. Scorn coated Rebecca's voice as she added, "Your people have been told and told and..."

Mr. Petrie sneered at her. "Miss Wilder, we have the leverage, not you. You're wasting—"

"Leverage, Mr. Petrie?" Slade Cordell sliced in, interposing his formidable authority.

The man rushed to justify his actions. "The report on the property, Wildjanna, indicates that it is mortgaged to the hilt. The owner will not be able to withstand—"

Rebecca's eyes flashed their angry frustration at Slade Cordell. "My grandmother has told your people over and over again. We are not selling! Neither she nor I will sell Wildjanna!"

Mr. Petrie snorted contempt at her assertion. "It can only be a matter of time. You're playing a fool's game. One old woman and a girl trying to run a place like that. You'll crack. Everyone does. And everyone has their price!"

Rebecca was on her feet before she knew it. Her hands were spread on the table, her body bent forward, words spitting off her tongue. "One old woman! That old woman, Mr. Petrie, could run rings around you. She and my grandfather pioneered that land. She'll die on that land where her husband and children have lived and died. Nothing you can do or say will ever shift her. Or me. It's our home, Mr. Petrie. And any time you want to step foot on it, that old woman and I will comprehensively show you how much of a fool's game we play."

She swept a scathing look around the rich room. "You sit up here in your little eyrie high above the real world and move your figures around like pieces in an elaborate chess game. All you do is flex the power that your money gives you. But money is only paper! Little bits of paper, or figures on a computer. And you can't touch us with money, Mr. Petrie. We're the backbone of this world. We're the earth, the producers on the land, the substance from which everything else takes its existence."

Petrie gave her a mocking clap. "That sounds fine, Miss Wilder. That's all it is. A fine sound. It won't help you when the bank forecloses on your property. Then you'll see how much paper money is worth," he jeered.

Rebecca's chin lifted in utter disdain for his claim. "There is not one bank in Australia that would foreclose on Wildjanna, Mr. Petrie. We are totally, irrevocably out of your reach!"

"We have ways and means to—"

"Mr. Petrie!" Slade Cordell's voice speared at his executive, steel-edged with the kind of command that would not brook defiance. "We will listen to what Miss Wilder has to say, Mr. Petrie. It appears to me that someone should have listened to Miss Wilder a long time ago. I would not care for another interruption, Mr. Petrie, so please don't speak again unless you're spoken to."

A rush of blood suffused Mr. Petrie's neck and cheeks with angry colour, but his lips tightened over the words he was bursting to say. The cold blue gaze of Slade Cordell dismissed him and returned to Rebecca.

"Now, Miss Wilder..." His voice resumed a polite and gently encouraging tone. "Would you kindly explain to me about no bank foreclosing?"

Rebecca was wary. She didn't know what to believe about Slade Cordell. Although he had just put his own man down in favour of hearing what she had to say, it was impossible to tell if he was playing a game or was deadly serious. Was he on her side? She wanted him to be. Suddenly she wanted that very much. A strong man, with the ultimate authority to crush anyone beneath him. She shivered at that thought then quickly concentrated her mind on the issue that had brought her to him.

This was the final showdown. She would leave no loopholes for any excuses not to do what should be done at Devil's Elbow. She met those compelling blue eyes with steely resolution.

"In our country, Mr. Cordell, it takes three generations to put a property where it is safe from all disasters. I'm the third generation at Wildjanna. It is true that we are mortgaged to the hilt at the moment. This is not at all unusual when times are as bad as these. We may lose most of our stock. We may go to the wall in every financial sense you like to think of. But if we go under, so would every other property owner in the north. So no bank will ever foreclose on us. The government wouldn't allow it to happen."

"Why are you so sure of that, Miss Wilder?" It was an inquisitive question, not inferring doubt, simply a request for elaboration.

Rebecca smiled, totally confident in her reply. "There's no one better equipped to recover the losses than we are, Mr.

Cordell. You see, the land always does recover. And in good times, the Channel Country can compete with the finest grazing lands in the world. If worse comes to worst, the government will always step in to help us. In our country, they don't have any other option.''

He nodded. While he was still weighing her words Rebecca spiked any misconception he might still be nursing. ''We will never sell, Mr. Cordell. When my grandmother dies, I inherit. If I die without children, the land is willed to the Aboriginal people who live on the station. They will never sell. They know too well what it's like to be a disinherited people. So even if my grandmother and I meet with some...unforeseen accident, Cordell Enterprises will not get its hands on Wildjanna. No matter what happens.''

His smile softened the ruthless cut of his face and lent it considerable charm. His eyes actually twinkled with amusement. Rebecca felt a strong pull of attraction. It was highly disconcerting. The last thing she had ever expected was to find Slade Cordell attractive in any way whatsoever.

''I would never wish an 'unforeseen accident' on you, Miss Wilder, but I have one hypothetical question. What if you marry?''

Rebecca knew in her heart she would never marry. Not unless Paul changed his mind, and then she would marry him. In the three years since he had broken their engagement, he had not shown the slightest wavering from his conviction that she must marry someone else, a man who could give her the kind of marriage she needed, the kind that he could no longer offer. Yet how could she ever do that? She owed him her love and loyalty...

''Miss Wilder?'' Slade Cordell asked softly.

She snapped out of her deep introspection. Slade Cordell was waiting for an answer. ''Should I ever marry, there'll be another man at Wildjanna," she stated unequivocally. "And a fourth generation."

That closed all the loopholes. The situation was now spelled out in capital letters. No mistakes could be made about it.

"Thank you for being so patient with me, Miss Wilder. I accept that as conclusive."

The gleam of intense satisfaction in his eyes suggested that Rebecca had given him the answer he wanted to hear. Although why that should be so, she couldn't imagine. He must be playing some deep game, she thought dismissively.

"Having now settled the question of tenure beyond any doubt," he continued smoothly, "I would like very much to get back to my original question. Please sit down and be comfortable, Miss Wilder. You were going to tell us why my cattle are going to die. It is a matter of considerable concern to me, a matter that both you and I want resolved. If you'd be so good as to oblige..."

Rebecca sat down again.

But didn't feel comfortable.

It seemed absurdly incongruous to even talk about cattle in this richly panelled room with its plush carpeting and the expensively suited men who were so sleekly tailored for international business. Everything about this place, these people, seemed far more than half a world away from home. It was a totally alien environment to her with no common reference point at all.

What could these men care about cattle? Beef prices yes, but hooves in the dust, the bellowing stampede to water, the plaintive bleat of calves left behind...what reality did that have in a room such as this? But if Slade Cordell wanted reality, she would give it to him.

"Water," she stated glumly. "We've had four years of drought, Mr. Cordell. My grandmother and I have done our best to keep the peace, but with the stock levels on your property so high—'' she shot a glare at Mr. Petrie ''—and kept deliberately high to pressure us, the situation is getting critical. If we keep watering your herd, Emilio Dalvarez will go short.''

''You mean Logan's Run doesn't control the water?'' Slade Cordell looked appalled.

''No, it doesn't, Mr. Cordell.'' It gave her a rich sense of satisfaction to drive this point home. ''That's why it's called Devil's Elbow. Was called Devil's Elbow before your organisation bought it four years ago. We control the water in times of drought.''

''You and your grandmother.''

''Wildjanna. Our property, Mr. Cordell. The creek dries up on your land first. Then on Emilio Dalvarez's land. Wildjanna has been the only cattle station in our area to hold water even through the worst droughts. And one of them lasted as long as seven years,'' she added, just to make sure he realised what might be in front of him. ''That could be another three years... or more.''

''Is Logan's... Devil's Elbow out of water now?'' he asked.

''Yes.''

Concern furrowed the wide brow and narrowed the blue eyes. ''Are we buying water from you?''

She gave him a scornful look. ''We don't sell water! That's not the way we do things in our part of the world, Mr. Cordell. Access to our water is freely given, but your people aren't playing by the rules. If you don't cut down on your stock, then we may all have to go short. For the first time in over sixty years we have to think about limiting your access.''

"You came six thousand miles to tell me this?" Slade Cordell inquired softly, his concern focused entirely on her now.

Rebecca's heart did a funny flip. He seemed to care... really care... yet how could he? But at least he was listening to her. She decided to ignore his expressions and simply lay out the facts.

"My grandmother and I decided you had to be told. Because the situation could turn very ugly if you don't act soon. Not only for us, Emilio—"

"Who is Emilio Dalvarez?"

"Our neighbour. He's an émigré Argentinian, and for all that he's been in Australia for thirty years, he's lost none of his Latin hot-bloodedness, nor his ingrained sense of honour. He can see as well as anyone what is happening and his sense of injustice is burning on a very short fuse."

"Where's his ranch?"

"To the west of Wildjanna. Your station, or ranch as you call it, is to the south. You and he share one common boundary. The altercations have already started. Emilio will resort to cutting down your herd with bullets if we don't come up with a satisfactory solution soon. As I said, we are doing our best to keep the peace, but your people have been less than co-operative, Mr. Cordell."

She finished on a note of intense bitterness. She had spent thousands of dollars in this last-ditch effort to get someone at Cordell Enterprises to see sense. And she hadn't liked leaving Gran to handle everything at home alone. Indomitable she might be, but she was old, and this last month had shortened Emilio Dalvarez's temper. Not that Gran would back off from using a shotgun if she had to. If only Pa hadn't died... Rebecca shook her head at the futile thought.

"I'm sorry you've been put to so much trouble on our account, Miss Wilder."

She looked up, startled not by the apology so much as the way he had seemed to read her thoughts. It gave her an odd, vulnerable feeling. "I've told you the truth, Mr. Cordell," she said sharply. "Take it or leave it. You have a week in which to act. If you don't, we will."

"Something will be done, Miss Wilder. Most assuredly so. I will see to it personally."

He sounded sincere but Rebecca had heard verbal assurances all week in these offices. They were meaningless. When the management at Devil's Elbow started moving stock to sale yards she would believe she had accomplished something, not before.

"I hope you do," she said wearily. It had been a long, hard week. She rose from the chair, tall, dignified and dismissive of all that Cordell Enterprises stood for. "I've had enough of this place, Mr. Cordell. I'm going home."

He was on his feet before she had even turned towards the door. And he was smiling at her again. Her heart fluttered. It must be because he's so big, Rebecca thought, although she wasn't the least bit nervous of him. She had no reason to be. She had truth, right and justice on her side.

"I think I might just come with you."

His voice wasn't a soft drawl this time. It resounded with a rich depth and was surprisingly pleasant. What he meant by his words was more obscure. Probably he was going to escort her out of the boardroom, out to the elevator. The look in his eyes suggested he admired her, or at least appreciated the presentation she had made of her case. He damned well should appreciate it, too, Rebecca reminded herself. It hadn't cost him a cent but it had cost her plenty.

"We are deeply in your debt," he continued, disconcerting her anew with his seeming ability to read her thoughts.

"Yes, you are," Rebecca said tartly. "I hope you remember it. Now, if you'll excuse me..."

"Of course. You've been more than generous with your time."

He strode down the room towards her, clearly intent on seeing her out. He certainly looked imposing in his three-piece suit. The fancy red and navy silk tie was a class touch on the pristine white shirt. He could well afford class, Rebecca thought cynically. He reached her side, and all she had done was turn towards him. She was tired. Worn out. Prey to all sorts of silly fancies. How could she even think that Slade Cordell was attractive? He was so different from Paul...

"Before you go home—"

"My return flight was booked before I came, Mr. Cordell," she said tersely, discomfited by the comparison she had just made. "I leave this afternoon from Kennedy Airport. I'm going now to pick up my luggage from my hotel and—"

"What time is your flight?" he cut in, his brows drawing together as if in displeasure.

"Four-fifteen."

He glanced at his watch. "I'll have someone take you to my office. Please wait there, Miss Wilder. I'll arrange a car for you. It's the least I can do."

Why not? Rebecca thought. It would save her some hefty taxi fares. "Very well. Thank you."

He smiled, satisfaction glinting in his eyes. Then he took her arm and led her out of the boardroom.

Rebecca was quite relieved to be handed over to someone else. Whether it was his size or the forcefulness of his character, she wasn't quite sure, but Slade Cordell certainly made his presence felt close up. Even his hand on her arm had a penetrating touch. She wanted to rub the feeling away when he released her but she controlled the urge. After all, she was never going to see him or be subjected to his presence again.

He had certainly treated her with courtesy. She had to say that for him. She hoped he was a man of integrity. If he kept his word that he would personally see to correcting the problem, then all the trouble would be over. Rebecca had no doubt about that. Slade Cordell was not the kind of man who tolerated anyone flouting his authority.

She wondered what it would be like to have a man like him at her side, a man who would not let anything beat him. A need stirred deep inside her. The need that Paul might have filled if the accident hadn't happened. Yet Paul hadn't had the invincible quality that emanated from Slade Cordell. The big American wouldn't have backed out of the life she offered just because he was tied to a wheelchair. He would have found a way to conquer whatever needed to be conquered.

Rebecca shook her head at such foolish whimsy. Slade Cordell was a city man. Not for him, her kind of life. And his kind of life was not for her. She was going home, away from his world. A long way away.

CHAPTER THREE

REBECCA CHECKED HER WATCH as she was ushered into Slade Cordell's office. Strange as it seemed—was it only an hour since she had decided she would barge in on Slade Cordell wherever he was?—it was only a few minutes past eleven. She had plenty of time to make it to the airport.

She refused the refreshments offered by her escort and was left alone. If she required anything, she was told, she only needed to press a button on the telephone and she would be given instant service. This was on a massive desk top of black marble, the focal dramatic feature of a vast room mostly furnished in blues and grays.

The decor was starkly modern—leather sofas, small tables made of slabs of marble balanced on polished chrome bases, glass shelves set on chrome structures and filled with books or graced with modern sculptures, which invited the eye to imagine what it liked. Rebecca wondered whether Slade Cordell had bought them himself or if they were simply the selection made by an expensive interior decorator.

The only thing she had no doubt about was the placement of the massive desk. Slade Cordell would certainly have ordered that. It was opposite the wall of plate glass, which presented a panoramic view of the city skyline. Since the office was situated on the thirty-fifth floor, this was something to behold, and Rebecca was sure it gave the head of Cordell Enterprises a feeling of enormous power.

She looked out on the thrusting concrete and glass skyscrapers of this mighty city and shuddered. How could people spend their lives in structures such as these, year after year? To her it was soulless. The huge monoliths of Manhattan were like monuments to some god that she couldn't worship. It was totally incomprehensible. Yet it existed, this life in the sky. Let them have it, she thought. I'll take the land.

She didn't know how long she stood there. She only knew that she belonged somewhere else, with red earth and grey-green trees and brilliant blue skies that could dazzle the eyes. A place where the sun both blistered and caressed with warmth, where water was a life-giving thing and unpolluted by chemicals, where people and animals knew their life cycle was bound to the land.

Her mind slowly drifted onto what would happen at home if Slade Cordell was as good as his word. Gran would be able to force Emilio to back off and keep to the course that she stipulated for getting through the drought. It would take some time for the ill will that had been generated to die down but they could weather that. All it took was resolution, and neither Gran nor she was about to cave in on anything.

The sound of the door opening startled her out of her intense reverie. She swung around and was even more startled to see Slade Cordell enter the room. "Is your board meeting over?" she asked, confused by his unexpected appearance.

"I've adjourned the meeting until further notice," he said, his eyes glinting with some secret triumph. "You've been enjoying the view?"

"I don't like it. It's not my world at all," she blurted out. "But I wish to thank you for hearing me out."

"The least I could do," he assured her.

Something fluttered between them—an empathy, a brief locking of souls. It was weird, unreal, and Rebecca forcefully rejected it. A city man like him . . . impossible! There wasn't one shred of compatibility to form the remotest link!

"I've made all the necessary arrangements for us," he said, coupling them together as if he hadn't rejected it at all. "If you'll give me the name of your hotel, your luggage will be picked up while we have lunch."

He stepped over to the desk and picked up the telephone receiver. "Your hotel?" he prompted softly.

Rebecca gave it somewhat stiffly, not at all sure that she wanted to have lunch with him. Slade Cordell's strong personality was a little too forceful for her liking, assuming an acceptance of an invitation that wasn't even offered.

On the other hand, if he wanted to pump her for more background information on the problems at home before she left New York, it would be stupid of her to begrudge him the opportunity. Besides, he was saving her considerable trouble, and undoubtedly he would insist on paying for lunch, as well. Another small recompense for the treatment she had suffered this week.

She watched him give instructions over the telephone, her mind preoccupied with eliminating any feeling of attraction towards him. He was certainly well-proportioned for his height. But that didn't make him any more of a man than Paul. It simply emphasized his maleness and gave an impression of powerful virility. Which could easily be false. As for his face . . .

Rebecca forgot about assessing Slade Cordell's face. His eyes were wandering over her, and not in the same kind of cool, testing appraisal he had made before. Every female instinct she had started prickling with sensitivity as his gaze lingered on the firm thrust of her breasts, then roved slowly down the curve of her hips to the long line of her legs, and even more slowly to the slim fineness of her ankles before skating back up to her face. The blue eyes reflected an intense inner satisfaction and Rebecca burnt with the knowledge that he had just measured her sexual appeal to himself and the answer he had come up with was extremely positive.

Rebecca was suddenly assailed by a mental image of what he might look like stripped of his ultra-civilised tailoring. What it might be like if... Another wave of heat raced through her veins as she clamped down on her crazy imaginings. She couldn't really want that! Not since the time of her engagement to Paul had she felt even a glimmer of sexual desire for a man. On the other hand, she hadn't met anyone quite like Slade Cordell.

Not that she would ever go to bed with him. He would only use her for his own private pleasure. However, Rebecca could not help wondering how good he was at giving that kind of pleasure. Except for Paul she might have been tempted. Even now... She put the thought behind her. Utter madness.

She was going home this afternoon, away from New York, away from Slade Cordell and his high-powered business world. Nevertheless, it gave her a deep satisfaction to know that the attraction she was feeling was not one-sided. Although it couldn't lead anywhere, the fact that Slade Cordell found her desirable was a flattering compliment to her femininity. A much nicer compliment than Emilio's reason for wanting the same thing.

Despite the fact that the Argentinian was twice Rebecca's age, Emilio Dalvarez had enough arrogance in his manliness to consider himself a suitable partner for her. He hadn't spoken yet, hadn't made a single move, but Rebecca was aware that he was considering it. There had been the odd testing comment about Paul, the occasional remark about

Wildjanna needing a man in charge. Emilio would like very much to be in control of Wildjanna. That would be far more important to him than having Rebecca share his bed. Whereas Slade Cordell . . .

He put down the telephone and started walking towards her.

Rebecca stiffened, appalled at the thought that he might have read her mind again. The way he had picked up on her thoughts before was positively uncanny. Embarrassment flooded through her, sharpened by a sense of disloyalty to the love that still bonded her to Paul.

There was a perceptive hesitation in his step, then he smoothly changed course, an affable smile breaking the intentness that had alarmed her. "Would you like me to close the curtains?" he asked with all the politeness of a considerate host. "Since you don't like the view," he added as Rebecca stared blankly at him.

"It doesn't matter. I'm going," she reminded him. And herself. This was his world and she wanted no part of it. Or him. This sexual speculation was a momentary aberration on both their parts. Quite clearly he had just dismissed it from his mind and she must dismiss it from hers.

"I'd like you to be comfortable while you're here. I've ordered lunch to be brought up," he informed her casually. "It saves us the bother of going to a restaurant and gives us more time to get to know each other better before we have to leave for the airport."

Rebecca's mind whirled into confusion again. "What do you mean, *we?* Are you taking me to the airport?" she asked, latching onto that point because the "getting to know each other" part was raising flutters in her stomach.

"As I said, I'm coming back to Australia with you. I'll make certain that the difficulties you have with Cordell Enterprises will be sorted out on the spot. I also wish to con-

vey my gratitude personally to your grandmother, and pay
my respects to her. She sounds just like someone else I used
to know. I also want to apologise to her for all the worry my
people have caused her.''

He was closing the curtains as he spoke, tossing the words
out in a matter-of-fact tone. It was not often that Rebecca
was struck speechless. She simply stared at him, unable to
believe he actually meant what he said.

He turned to her with an ironic little smile that she
couldn't read at all. ''You see, Miss Wilder,'' he said in his
soft Texas drawl, ''there are people in this country who are
just like yours. And we don't like to see cattle suffer, either.''

The shock of Slade Cordell's calmly spoken announcement was compounded by the realisation that he was completely serious. The slight smile on his lips was not echoed
in his eyes. Those dark blue eyes held an intensity of purpose, a firmness of resolution that would allow nothing and
no one to get in his way.

''That's very handsome of you, Mr. Cordell,'' Rebecca
said dazedly. And even that was an understatement. For him
to drop everything else to take a personal hand in sorting out
a problem on the outermost perimeter of his business empire...

''Let's make it Slade,'' he said, and there was nothing
unreadable about his smile this time. It was one-hundred-
percent charm—open, warm, friendly, appealing—demol-
ishing at one stroke the barriers of culture, background,
status and any other differences between them. Except the
one elementary difference that he was a man and she was a
woman. The smile did a fine job of emphasising that basic
point.

''Are you called Rebecca, or do you prefer some shortened version of your name?'' he asked, pressing for the fa-

miliarity in a way that made rejection of it seem totally churlish.

"Rebecca," she replied, feeling hopelessly confused by what he was projecting. He wouldn't go so far, do something so extreme, just because he felt attracted to her, would he? "Surely it's inconveniencing you a great deal to break off your business to accompany me," she said in an attempt to probe his motives.

"This *is* my business," he returned softly. "And it inconvenienced you and your grandmother a great deal more to bring the matter to my attention, Rebecca."

"But..." She floundered under the disturbing intentness in his eyes. She couldn't really believe this concentrated interest in her. He couldn't really care about her. "My grandmother will welcome you," she finished limply, certain of nothing except that this was a result she had never envisaged in her list of possibilities.

"I'm counting on that," he said, and his eyes gleamed with a private satisfaction that suggested he had more on his mind than making peace. "Come. Sit down and relax," he invited, waving towards a conversational grouping of leather sofas. "I want to know a lot more about what I'm likely to meet at Devil's Elbow."

Rebecca accepted the invitation to sit down but she did not relax. He settled on the sofa facing her, but even with a table between them, Slade Cordell's strong presence aroused a tension in her that she couldn't dispel. She wasn't used to men like him, men who did as they liked and didn't count the cost. Perhaps that was an exaggeration. A person in his position had to calculate costs, but in this instance he had decided to disregard them. Or whatever it was he wanted was worth any cost at all.

"Have you had some personal involvement with cattle, Mr. Cordell?" she asked, forcing her mind onto business.

It was difficult to suppress the treacherous feeling of excitement building from the thought that she would be seeing a lot more of this man.

He gave her a teasing little smile. "Am I so old to you that you can't bring yourself to call me Slade? Or have you thought of me as the enemy so long that it's impossible to accept the goodwill of a friendly overture?"

"Not at all," she countered quickly, anxious to hide the fact that her pulse was acting erratically. "Slade is fine." She managed an ironic smile. "My mind is a little slow in making the adjustment, but I assure you that any friendly overture is very definitely welcomed."

"I'm glad that's settled." He heaved a sigh and shot her a look that begged forgiveness. "I'm sorry you had to deal with Dan Petrie, but if it gives you any satisfaction, you nailed his coffin this morning. He's out. And he won't be the only one to go, either."

A grim look of resolution settled on his face. "I'm going to have to rejuvenate Cordell Enterprises. It's got top-heavy. When it starts spawning men like Dan Petrie..."

His business life was all so totally foreign to Rebecca. She lifted her gaze to the curtains that hid the view of his world. But it was there, just behind them. That was his reality. She shouldn't have let him close those curtains. Somehow it had shifted the ground between them, closing a distance that was really unbridgeable.

He brightened again, sending her a smile that bridged all distances. "I'm like you, Rebecca," he said, the blue eyes projecting an intimate understanding. "We share the doubtful honour of being the last of our line. Except I don't have a grandparent left alive."

He wasn't like her, Rebecca told herself fiercely, and he had no right to be suggesting he was, no right to stir feelings in her that suggested possibilities that were impossibilities.

"You aren't married?" she asked. There had to be some woman in his life. A man like him had to have any number of city women hanging around him, even if he wasn't married.

His smile gathered a touch of smugness. "No attachment at all," he replied.

"Why not?" Rebecca demanded. It was unreasonable for him to be still single, a man in his mid-thirties. It wasn't as if he had no choice over whom to marry. *He* wasn't being forced by circumstances into a limbo state of loneliness.

He shrugged. "Perhaps I haven't found a woman I'd care to keep at my side."

Her green eyes mocked such a contention. "You must be a very demanding man, then."

"Yes," he agreed, looking at her with flattering speculation, subtly challenging her to be the one he would want to keep at his side.

Rebecca mentally recoiled from the flirtation. He was playing a game with her. As he probably did with any woman whom he found passably attractive. Rebecca was not interested in that type of game. It was cynical and heartless, particularly since he knew as well as she did that their lives couldn't mix. An interesting little affair—that was what he was contemplating, wanting from her. He would never stand at her side or be there for her when she needed him to be.

"Don't you want children?" she asked, more to probe his character than from any personal interest.

"I don't have a dynastic urge. If I die without having children—" a look of sardonic weariness dragged over his features "—what the heck does it matter! There are more

than enough children in this world to be fed and cared for
without my adding to the overpopulation problem.''

Rebecca made no comment. Whether he was really concerned about the children of the world she could not tell, but
he obviously didn't care about having children of his own.

''You look sad,'' he said softly.

Rebecca flicked her gaze to his. He had been studying her
again. ''I'm not like you, Slade,'' she said, wanting to es-
tablish that fact in his mind as well as her own.

Children were important to her... another generation.
Paul knew that. Paul—an anguished sense of loss twisted
through her. She had shared her dreams with him, shared
everything with him, things that Slade Cordell would never
know or value.

Their lunch arrived, wheeled in on a trolley. As far as
Rebecca was concerned, it came none too soon. Slade Cordell was a dangerous man, dangerous to her sense of right
and wrong. While a table was being set with the meal, she
worked hard at getting her mind fixed in a purely business
mode.

Slade Cordell was accompanying her to Australia. She
had to ensure it was for one purpose only, to push the necessary restraints onto the management at Devil's Elbow. She
and her grandmother would extend him every courtesy
warranted in the circumstances. That was it. If he wanted
more, that was his problem, not hers.

Logic, however, was a poor force against the big American's attractions. Apart from his strong physical impact,
which seemed to get stronger by the minute, he was most
attentive to everything she said, and occasionally there were
those flashes of charm that begged a response from her.
Rebecca struggled to fight off their treacherous effect.

After lunch they travelled to Kennedy Airport in a stretch
limousine. Rebecca appreciated the extra room in the stately

car. It meant she could put some seat distance between her and the man next to her. She found his physical closeness intensely disturbing.

At least she wouldn't be sitting with him on the flight, she assured herself. Her ticket was for economy class and she was absolutely certain that Slade Cordell would never fly that way.

However, when they arrived at the airport, Rebecca found that she had underestimated Slade Cordell's "arrangements" for her. Her ticket was exchanged for a first-class one, at the expense of Cordell Enterprises. She could hardly protest Slade's argument that they owed it to her. And much more besides. The cost of her trip to New York would be reimbursed. He regretted that he could not make up for all the time wasted and stress caused by misdirected employees of his organisation. His apologetic concern appeared to be so genuine that even Rebecca's pride in her own independence was disarmed.

He was subtly but relentlessly moving in on her. Rebecca knew it. Yet she didn't seem able to stop him. There was nothing overt—a smile, a courteous touch on her arm, every word to her perfectly straightforward—yet she was beginning to feel hunted by a very experienced hunter.

Slade steered her to the first-class lounge to await their flight call, and Rebecca took the opportunity to escape his disturbing presence for a while. Having reclaimed her smaller bag from the luggage that had been waiting to be checked through, she took advantage of the luxurious amenities of the ladies' room to change out of her good clothes and into a more comfortable travelling outfit.

The stretch jeans, white T-shirt and denim jacket she had set apart for this purpose might not look first-class, but the need to impress anyone was past as far as she was concerned. Practical and comfortable, she thought, and a far cry from the elegant sophistication that Slade Cordell would be used to in his women.

Having packed away the coral suit and its attendant finery, Rebecca stood in front of the vanity and unpinned her hair. The thick black mass of it tumbled down her back. She brushed it out, gathered it with her hands, then slid a hair grip around it at the nape of her neck.

She examined her reflected image, wondering what Slade Cordell saw in her. She simply couldn't comprehend why he would go so far to make a conquest of any woman, let alone a woman with whom he had nothing in common. Surely she had to be imagining his personal interest in her. Yet there was something in those compelling blue eyes that kept telling her she was not being fanciful.

Rebecca did her best to shrug off the disturbing speculation. She was going home—home to Wildjanna—and she had done what she had come to do in New York. With more success than she had ever believed possible. She didn't want Slade Cordell to be attracted to her any more than she wanted to feel attracted to him. There was no future in it. None at all.

Having steeled herself to keep a firm distance between them, Rebecca returned to the lounge. She was surprised to see Slade had also changed his clothes for a more casual outfit, although the soft supple grey leather jacket, crisp white sports shirt and beautifully tailored grey slacks were a long way from being off-the-peg garments. Rebecca suspected he would cut an impressive figure even in the cheapest, shabbiest clothes procurable. When he stood up at her entrance, she had the craven wish that he was someone other than who he was, someone who had been born and bred to share her kind of life.

She avoided meeting those dark blue eyes that were far too perceptive for her liking. She would have sat down and picked up a magazine to pass the waiting time except he stepped forward and forestalled her, one hand lightly grasping her arm, its warmth and strength seeping through her jacket sleeve and forcing her to look at him.

The expression on his face was grim. He looked older than she had previously thought, as though his years suddenly sat heavily on him. And his eyes, why were they probing hers so anxiously?

"Rebecca, a message has just come through for you from your hotel," he said quietly, his voice low and strained.

Whether it was the change in his manner or the beginning of a terrible premonition, Rebecca didn't know, but she felt an odd tightening of her heart.

"A message from my grandmother?" she asked. Some new trouble, she thought. Had Emilio broken the agreement?

"No, it's not from your grandmother, Rebecca. It's to say..." He hesitated, torn between the desire to soften the news and the knowledge that he was the last person in the world who could soften it. "You'd better read it, Rebecca."

He lifted his other hand, offering her the slip of paper he had held out of sight until now. Rebecca almost snatched it from him, impatient to know whatever it was she had to know. Her eyes leapt to the top of the printed message, expecting to read of some urgent problem on Wildjanna but the letters spelled out other words, words that hammered into her heart and broke something there.

Your grandmother passed away this morning.

She stared at the flimsy sheet of paper, her mind reading its message over and over again as though what was spelled out had to change into something else if she kept studying it, but it didn't change, and her mind finally had to accept the impact that had already broken something in her heart.

Broken something and let in a searing sense of loneliness, bereftness, as if her whole world had disappeared and she stood on a tiny pinnacle on top of a terrible void.

"Rebecca..." The soft call of her name reached her from a far distance.

She slowly lifted her gaze and saw a man looking at her with deep concern. Slade Cordell, her mind registered sluggishly. Slade Cordell of Cordell Enterprises. Gran had entrusted her with the mission of telling him what he had to be told. And here she was in New York—this terrible, soulless place—so far away, a world away from all that meant anything to her. While she had been here running around in futile circles, Gran... Gran...

It was *his* fault. But for this man and his damnable organisation she would have been home where she belonged. The drought would have been just another drought to be weathered. Gran would not have been so pressured or driven to expend so much of her strength in holding the peace. It was no excuse that he didn't know what was going on. He should have known. Should have stopped it. It was too late to make amends now. Too late...

Then the mantle of Janet Wilder settled on her granddaughter's shoulders. Rebecca's spine stiffened. Purpose and resolution hardened the green eyes. Pain, no matter how bad, had to be endured, put aside until there was time to work through it. No matter what the rights or wrongs of the situation, there was a tradition to be upheld. Wildjanna needed someone in control. There were things that had to be done.

Slade watched the emergence of Rebecca Wilder from deep shock with a sense of awe. He had watched the blood drain from her face, the frightening, trancelike state that had followed. He desperately wanted to reach out to her, to help, to comfort, but he knew that any such gesture from him could only be rejected.

Then the blind bitter hatred he had feared—and probably deserved—had flashed out at him, brief, intense and firmly suppressed. The recovery of the woman, the burning inner strength that rose out of the ashes of nothingness was little short of incredible for one as young as she.

In the boardroom he had thought she was a woman of remarkable mettle, but even that had been an underestimation of her character. There was an air of majesty about her now, of a queen mounting the throne for the first time, girding herself for the task ahead, whatever that entailed.

An eerie feeling of premonition crawled down Slade's spine. His intuition about Rebecca Wilder had been right. She was capable of anything. Anything! He hadn't fully realised that potential in her.

She had thrown out a challenge that had excited him, fired his blood. The way she had attacked Dan Petrie, the almost primitive savagery of her spirit, the magnificent disdain for all he himself represented . . . Slade had never met that before. Never! The urge to tame her, to win her surrender...that, he'd been certain, would be an experience worth having.

Now he wasn't sure if in winning what he wanted, he might also end up losing more than he won. Yet somehow there was an even greater fascination in going on. The extra barrier of her grandmother's death made it a lot harder, but no, he couldn't back away now. He didn't want to back away.

"You've read this?" she asked, her ageless face strikingly set in lines of unbreakable strength.

"Yes. I'm sorry, Rebecca." He knew she wouldn't want his sympathy, but what else could he say?

"We have run out of time," she stated, her eyes clear and steady and determined. "If you care about your cattle I suggest you get a message through to your people on Devil's Elbow straight away. Tell them to keep their herd away from Wildjanna until we get there. It won't hurt the cattle to go thirsty for a day or two."

"That's no problem," he assured her. "But why the urgency? We'll be there—"

"Emilio will take revenge," she cut in. "That's his nature. He'll be looking for any excuse to start blasting at your cattle or your people."

The green eyes looked through him, seeing a past or a future that Slade had no part of. "Emilio Dalvarez revered my grandmother. She ruled Wildjanna. And in doing so, she commanded his respect and forbearance. Those checks are now gone and his outrage at your people will be immeasurably deepened. He will feel justified in taking matters into his own hands. Only I can stop him now, and it will be at least another day before I can get home."

"Rebecca . . ."

Her focus snapped to him. "My grandmother is dead, Slade. You caused it. Indirectly it may be, but you and your organisation caused it."

There was nothing Slade could say to that. He nodded mute agreement, wishing he could take her in his arms, wishing he could offer her some comfort. He didn't dare try. Certainly she had felt an attraction towards him, but he was back to being the enemy again. Only time would make up the ground he had lost.

"I'll go and give the order. Make it top priority. They'll get the word at Devil's Elbow," he promised her. There was nothing else he could say to Rebecca Wilder at this point, but he was going to say one hell of a lot to his own people. *One hell of a lot!*

Rebecca watched him go to a small annex of the lounge where there were a number of telephones and fax machines. The pain and grief she felt welled up inside her, but she clamped down on them again. This was not the time or the place. She could not allow any sign of weakness. The tears and the deep sense of loss would come later when it was private and she could bury herself in her misery. There were too many things to be done first, too many things that had to be decided.

Beyond the shock and inner grief was also one driving certainty. It was the inexorable law of the land. After death came the regeneration, the inevitable cycle of life. No matter what Paul could or could not do, what he would or would not do, the death of her grandmother changed everything. From deep down in her soul Rebecca Wilder dredged up the one fundamental elemental decision.

There would be a fourth generation at Wildjanna.

CHAPTER FOUR

THEY BOARDED THE PLANE at the scheduled time, but take-off was delayed so long Rebecca grew increasingly fretful. She hated flying at the best of times, and this was certainly the worst. Apart from which she didn't like the look of the plane, either. The first-class compartment seemed small and cramped.

She closed her eyes, sick with nervous tension, sick at heart. If only she had done things differently, she could have been home sooner. She might have been able to do something for Gran, save her from dying, or at least been there to...to just be with her, to hold her hand and tell her all the unspoken heartfelt things that were taken so much for granted.

She shouldn't have let all those people at Cordell Enterprises give her the runaround for days on end. She should have.... But it was no use feeling guilty now. It was too late to change anything. She could no more go back in time than she could push this dreadful plane forward in time.

They finally started to move. The noise in the cabin increased. Rebecca shut her eyes tighter and prayed that they would lift safely off the ground. The plane was still shuddering when a warm hand curled over her clenched grip on the armrest.

"It's all right, Rebecca," came the soft reassurance from Slade Cordell. "We're off the ground and it's all systems go."

His concern, his kindness tapped into the weakness she was desperately trying to keep at bay. She felt tears prick her eyes and kept her lids shut until she could manage to force the tears back. She wanted someone to hold her hand, to share the burden that Gran's death left upon her shoulders, to comfort the awful aching loneliness. Slade Cordell's hand was strong...but it would soon be taken away. To start leaning on him in any way would only sap the will she had to find to carry on alone.

He didn't care about her. Not really. Perhaps some sympathy for her loss, but she didn't want his sympathy. She opened her eyes and flashed him a hard look. She didn't want anything from Slade Cordell except that he do what should have been done by Cordell Enterprises a long time ago. This whole trip had been so wasteful.

"I'll feel a lot better when we swap over to Qantas at Los Angeles," she said tersely. She hoped she didn't sound too xenophobic.

He nodded, smoothly removing his hand from hers. "And I guess you want to be with your own people."

She didn't want to give offence, and it was pointless to state that Qantas was the second-oldest airline in the world, with the best safety record in the world. The last time there had been a serious accident was in 1947.

His mouth twisted into an apologetic grimace. "I guess you haven't had much reason to like anything American."

Rebecca felt a twinge of guilt at her manner towards him. For whatever reason he had chosen to do it, he was going to be on hand to solve the worst problem she had to face. She had to be grateful for that large mercy.

"I wouldn't make a blanket judgement from this trip," she said flatly. Then, because she wasn't ready to cope with any idle conversation, she turned away from him to stare out the window.

They had to fly across the continent of North America. Rebecca had no doubt that somewhere down there were people she would like, people who shared the same values as herself. In fact, most of the Americans she had met were very likeable. They were friendly, warm, hospitable people, extremely courteous and helpful—except those who had been ordered not to be helpful, and that wouldn't have been their fault.

No, she had no prejudice against Americans, only against those who worshipped at the shrine of the almighty dollar, and people like that could be found in every nation of the world. She had met plenty of Australians who were contaminated with the same disease.

The hours passed slowly. Rebecca rejected the meal offered to her. A movie was shown but she didn't bother with the earphones. There was no escape from the devastating reality of her grandmother's death. The picture on the screen was meaningless.

A continuous stream of passengers got up to use the telephones fixed to the cabin walls across from the galley. Rebecca wondered whom they were calling—business contacts, friends, family? I'm the last of our line now, she thought desolately. Just like Slade Cordell. But unlike him, she couldn't and wouldn't let it stay that way. Wildjanna demanded continuation. Too much of her family's lifeblood had been poured into it to let it fall into other hands.

Slade made no further attempt at conversation, perhaps recognising that there was nothing he could say or do. She appreciated his tact in remaining silent. It surprised her that he was sensitive to her feelings. Then she remembered how he had seemed to read her mind and realised that he was more perceptive than most people. It wasn't that he cared. He simply knew when to push and when not to push. She supposed that was one of the qualities a man had to have to head an organisation as vast as Cordell Enterprises.

Certainly, if he did have any designs on her personally, he knew this was not the time to push them. He was, after all, virtually a stranger. Not even a friend. Yet oddly enough, she was glad he was sitting next to her. Strong silent company was better than no company at all while she endured this long flight home. She knew she had his support, although she suspected there was a price to be paid for it...if he had his way.

They were held up again on the tarmac at Los Angeles, but at least this time they were sitting in the extended luxury cabin of a Boeing 747 and Rebecca was more philosophical about the delay. The first-class accommodation was more spacious on this larger plane, the seats more comfortable, the service more attentive, and she couldn't help feeling a gratified pride in the Australian national airline.

However there were still another fifteen hours of flying to get through. It seemed to take forever before they left Los Angeles behind and headed out over the Pacific Ocean. Rebecca was about to wave away the offer of another meal but Slade interjected this time.

"You'll feel better—you'll sleep better—if you eat something Rebecca. At least try it," he advised.

She privately acknowledged he had a valid point, so she forced herself to eat as much as she could, although she had little appetite for the fine food set before her. Afterwards she did feel better. She was even more grateful to Slade for the first-class seat since it allowed her to stretch out and rest comfortably. She slept for the rest of the way to Hawaii, and for the last leg of the flight to Brisbane.

She did not stir until the announcement that breakfast would shortly be served. They had crossed the international date line, which meant they had lost all of Saturday, and it would be early Sunday morning when they arrived in Brisbane. Already Rebecca's biological clock was misfunctioning. She felt drained, tired and listless. It was more than likely shock had something to do with it, she reasoned, but the thought did nothing to revive her.

As she rose to go to the washroom to freshen up she noticed that Slade Cordell was clean-shaven and obviously ready to face the day ahead of them. She gave him a stiff little nod in response to his soft inquiry if she wanted a wake-up coffee. It was waiting for her when she returned to her seat and she sipped it gratefully.

"Rebecca, I don't want to distress you, but..." He looked searchingly into her eyes, looking for acceptance and finding it, although it was given with wary reservation.

"What do you want to say, Slade?"

He lifted an open hand in an appealing gesture. "I've organised a light aircraft at Brisbane Airport to fly me to Devil's Elbow. I don't know if you've made other travelling arrangements, but I thought, if you accompanied me, we could get things straightened out as soon as we arrive," he said persuasively.

The plan had been for her to take Monday's mail plane to get home, but that was no longer practical under the present emergency. An appreciative little smile hovered on her lips. When Slade Cordell moved, he certainly moved with efficient effectiveness. He was looking after her needs in a way that she wished... But it wasn't because he cared, Rebecca told herself sternly. It was simply his way of doing things. Control. Authority. A man used to being in command of himself and others. In deferring to her opinion, he was simply being tactful to suit the circumstances.

Rebecca nodded her consent. "Thank you. That will suit me fine."

"About your grandmother..." Slade hesitated, seeing the smile disappear and the sharp recoil in her eyes. He was wary of giving any offence. "I just thought...are there any arrangements I can make?"

She shook her head, poignantly aware of the medical and legal procedures that would already be in place. As with Pa, the flying padre would bring Gran back home to be buried on Wildjanna.

"We look after our own," she said simply.

There was a pattern to her life—a pattern to the land— that even Slade Cordell's power and authority couldn't touch. The thought of him confronting the Australian outback gave Rebecca a certain grim satisfaction. He would find her world as alien to him as she had found his. There he would be reduced to the same level as everyone else—a man who had to accept the terms the land forced upon him.

She wondered how he would stand up to it, then decided his stay would be so brief that it would not constitute anything more than a different experience. He could never be the one to stand at her side. For all his aura of being an invincible conqueror, he simply didn't know...what she knew.

An hour later the plane touched down on Australian soil. Rebecca was again grateful for the advantage of being a first-class passenger. She and Slade were amongst the first to disembark, and they moved through the arrival gates without having to queue. Their luggage appeared on the carousel at the second rotation, and again there was no queueing to get past the customs people. They were through the whole arrival process in half the time Rebecca had anticipated.

She was not expecting anyone to meet her. Her whole focus was on getting to Wildjanna. Slade was paged from the inquiries desk. As they moved in that direction, Rebecca's eye caught a wheelchair coming towards her. That something broken in her heart savaged her again. She couldn't bear to look at the occupant, to be reminded . . .

"Rebecca."

Paul's voice. Paul! She turned incredulously. Slade Cordell was instantly forgotten. Her eyes fastened on the face of the man to whom she had pledged her love, and clung with a bittersweet mixture of despair and hope. It had been a year since she had seen him, a year of dark yearning for things to be different. But he had come to be with her now, come for her in her time of need.

"Paul . . ." Her voice was a bare husky croak, shriven by turbulent emotions that had burst from her control.

His sun-streaked hair had darkened from being indoors instead of where he belonged. His handsome face was thinner, marked by suffering that he shared with no one. The warm brown eyes were filled with painful compassion.

Rebecca moved towards him without a thought for the man she left without a look or a word. Her hand slid into the hand outstretched to her and gripped tight. Tears blurred her eyes.

"You know about Gran?" she whispered.

"Milly called me," he answered quietly.

That was the housekeeper who had served her grandmother since before Rebecca was born, who had seen the growth of the relationship between her and Paul, who had shared its tragic outcome and wept over it with her.

"Your grandmother was a great lady, Rebecca. I know how much you'll miss her. How much she meant to you. I'm so sorry."

That was Paul, considering only her, never himself. "Paul—" she swallowed hard, fighting to get some steadiness back in her voice "—marry me, Paul. Please, marry me. Reconsider . . ."

The flash of deep inner anguish she saw in his eyes silenced the words that still trembled on her tongue, aching to be said.

"No!" His thumb kneaded the back of her hand. "I realise you're tired, Rebecca. Overwrought..."

"It's not that! It's not!" She fell to her knees beside him, openly begging as she forced out the words that had to be spoken. "I need you now. Like I've never needed you before."

"No...no..." His head jerked away then snapped back again, his eyes as agonised as hers yet burning with fevered resolution. "It's not my life any more, Rebecca. You have to accept that."

"I need you, Paul," she pleaded.

"Rebecca..." He spoke her name as though it embodied the whole loss of every promise there had ever been, echoing into an irrecoverable past. He reached out his other hand and gently smudged away the tears that had spilled from her lashes. "I'll always be here for you when you need me, but I'll never marry you. Please understand that, Rebecca. Never."

Her mind sought frantically for some other way to reach past the barrier of his making, not hers. It wasn't fair! It wasn't right! She shook her head in helpless denial of what was happening to her.

"Don't look back, Rebecca," Paul said quietly. His hand slid down to her chin and tilted her face up to his. "Now, more than ever, you must look forward. You know you can always count on me to stand by you as a friend."

A friend! Rebecca bit her lips. She didn't want him as a friend. She wanted, needed to have him beside her always. Why couldn't he see that?

She stared past him blindly, still inwardly fighting Paul's edict. It came as a sickening jolt when she realised that Slade

Cordell was staring at her, his vivid blue eyes ablaze with a stomach-twisting hunger.

Rebecca wrenched her gaze from his and struggled to her feet, torn between the mortifying thought that Slade had seen the baring of her soul and her need for Paul to respond to it. Yet when she looked at Paul again, she knew she had lost him. He had himself completely in control, his eyes steady with purpose, his chin set with determination.

"Milly also told me about the problem you're having with Cordell Enterprises, Rebecca," he said earnestly. "Don't worry about them. I'll put together a battery of lawyers that will keep them in legal tangles for years to come."

"No, Paul. I'm getting that problem sorted out." She didn't want to introduce Slade to Paul. Somehow it didn't seem right. Paul might look at Slade and see . . . Rebecca wasn't sure what it was he would see, but Slade Cordell was so much a man that it might make Paul feel less. And that was wrong.

"I can help you financially, Rebecca," Paul assured her. "I'm doing really well now. I can afford it. For the first time last year our profits exceeded ten million dollars. We're going after the big time and we're going to get it. . . ."

Money! What did money matter? Her eyes stabbed one last desperate appeal. "Marry me, Paul, and come back to Wildjanna!"

His gaze returned hers with resolute steadiness. "I've got a new life. I know it's not yours, Rebecca. And yours isn't mine any more. You are what you are, a worthy successor to your grandmother," he said firmly, decisively. "You have a path to follow. That's given to very few people in this world. I wish you well." He squeezed her hand. "If you want me to come with you to Wildjanna, to see you through . . ."

"No." That was too hard to accept, half a loaf that was no loaf at all. "I'll manage, Paul. I'm glad to hear you're doing so well. And thank you for coming to see me."

"That's what friends are for," he said softly.

"Yes. We're only friends," she whispered in painful resignation. He didn't love her. Not as she needed to be loved. He couldn't turn away from her now, when she so desperately needed him at her side, if he truly loved her. He had been separating himself from her ever since the accident, forging his new life without her, refusing to let her come to him.

"Always friends," he promised firmly. "Do you have some form of transport waiting for you?"

"Yes."

He nodded. "If there's anything I can do, call me."

"Thank you."

"Take care, Rebecca."

"You too, Paul."

She gave his hand a quick squeeze then turned away, walking blindly to Slade Cordell and the future that Paul would never share. He could have done it, if he'd wanted to enough. It simply didn't suit him any more. A different life, a different life.... The words hammered through Rebecca's heart.

She felt betrayed.

This was her darkest hour of need. She had been there at the hospital for Paul, offering him everything she was in his darkest hour of need. He had rejected her then and he had rejected her now. He hadn't been self-sacrificing at all in relinquishing his claim on her. It was Rebecca he had sacrificed, to follow a course that would fulfil his new needs. All this time, three years, and she had been yearning for something that was gone, that had never really been.

She had no one. No one but herself. She had to carry on alone.

"Does your friend need any assistance?" Slade asked, frowning over her shoulder.

"No." Rebecca did not look back. She knew that Paul would already be directing the wheelchair out of the airport terminal. A car, especially adjusted for the handicapped, would be waiting for him. He took pride in being totally independent.

She turned bleak, empty eyes to Slade Cordell. "There is a limit to what you can do with money."

It couldn't buy love. It couldn't mend what was irreparable. It couldn't buy back what was forever gone.

Gran was gone from her life.

Paul would only ever be a friend on the perimeter of her real existence.

That existence had begun and would end with Wildjanna. She had a path to follow and nothing—no one—was ever going to change that. It was imprinted too deeply on her soul. Paul had wanted to share it before the accident. He had said he loved her. But he couldn't have, Rebecca finally realised. Not deep-down love. Not life-commitment love. Because nothing should have changed. Just because he couldn't do what he had done before, he had sought a different life without her.

"You are what you are, Rebecca . . ." and he didn't want what she was any more.

A wave of tortured emotion swept through her, draining her of all strength. A hand clutched her arm as she swayed from faintness, a strong hand, giving her enough support to recollect herself.

"Would you like to sit? We'll have a coffee before—"

"No!" She forced herself to meet the concern in Slade Cordell's eyes. Temporary concern. It sickened her further because she needed so much more. So much, and Slade wouldn't give it any more than Paul would. "We have to move on!" she said grimly.

Don't look back, Rebecca. You must look forward.

"Are you sure?"

"Yes. I'm sure."

You have a path to follow...

CHAPTER FIVE

SLADE'S ADMIRATION for Rebecca Wilder's strength of character was mixed with an even deeper frustration. He had felt acutely envious of that man in the wheelchair. The way their hands had gripped, the sharing of emotion that Slade himself had been excluded from. Not that he could expect anything else. Rebecca Wilder had no reason to like him, let alone...

He tried to shrug off the feelings she was stirring in him. He had to get her on the plane that was waiting for them, get her home. It was a hell of a thing to have happened, her grandmother dying at such a time.

He had known that terrible feeling of bereftness when Grandfather Logan had died, the sense of loss, of a void that could never be filled by anyone else. It took time to get over it, time Slade knew he didn't have. But he would make it. Somehow he would get over that hurdle. And every other hurdle, too!

He held onto Rebecca's arm as he led her out of the international terminal and signalled a taxi. Despite the fire of resolution in her eyes, she looked so pale and withdrawn that Slade didn't want to remove this minimal support. He was relieved that she didn't spurn it, yet it disturbed him that she no longer seemed to have any awareness of him.

She certainly had passion. He had been right about that. Although he hadn't liked seeing the intense naked emotion that had been drawn from her by that man in the wheelchair. Slade wanted to ask her about him. It was difficult to restrain the urge to find out where the man fitted into her life. But he had no doubt such personal questions would not be welcomed. Not right now, anyway.

He settled her in the taxi and gave instructions to the driver. It was only a matter of minutes before they were delivered to the section of the airport that handled light aircraft. The chartered pilot was waiting for them as arranged. After introducing himself he took charge of their luggage and led them to a six-seater plane, which had the stylish lines of a recent model.

A Piper Navajo, the pilot informed Slade, as he cheerfully stowed the luggage on board through a cargo door. He was obviously a talkative guy, and after the long silence Slade had maintained with Rebecca, it was something of a relief to chat innocuously with a friendly person.

Rebecca had completely withdrawn inside herself. Sensitive to her need for privacy, Slade once again quelled his mounting frustration and accepted the pilot's invitation to sit beside him in the cockpit. Perhaps after a couple of hours in the air Rebecca might submit to a conversation with him, but he was wary of pressing his company on her until he saw some chance of her accepting it.

That man in the wheelchair had hurt her. She had taken it on the chin and risen above it, but she had definitely been hurt. Slade fiercely wanted to fill the bleak emptiness he had seen in her eyes with something positive—positive towards him—but there could be no forcing anything from Rebecca Wilder. Anything he got from her would be hard won. Slade had no delusions about that. But he wasn't giving up.

"Have you ever flown to Devil's Elbow before?" he asked the pilot as they lifted off the tarmac.

"Never landed there, but I've been over it a few times." He threw Slade a friendly grin. "We get a fair few tourists who want to have a look at outback stations. The Channel Country is a good place to show them. The sheer size of those properties always boggles their minds. Thousands of square miles, homesteads that look like small towns..."

"Have you got a map that I can follow as we fly?" Slade was interested to know more about this country that had given birth to a woman like Rebecca Wilder.

"Sure thing!" The pilot happily complied.

The map was old and deeply creased and somewhat grubby. Slade spread it out and the pilot pointed out various features.

"First we go over the Great Dividing Range, then across the Darling Downs—best grazing lands in the world when we're not in drought—*they* sure need rain pretty bad right now." He dragged his finger across to the southwest corner of Queensland. "Here's Devil's Elbow. We've got a few hours' flying ahead of us."

Slade looked down at the tiny print that located his property, then found Wildjanna to the north of it. "Devil's Elbow was renamed Logan's Run four years ago," he said in ironic comment.

"Is that a fact?" The pilot looked surprised. "Well, I guess I'll just stick to the old name. It's got more local colour. See how the creek on it bends like an elbow? That's Windy Drop-Down Creek. For some geological reason the creek bed drops to a much deeper level on the adjoining property, and the water just dries up on Devil's Elbow when a big drought hits. But I guess you know all about that?"

"Yep. The situation is pretty bad," Slade agreed. "And I'm going to fix it."

He glanced at Rebecca but she was not listening to them. She was closed into some tight inner world that was hers and hers alone. The strange thing was, Slade reflected, she continually made him feel he was missing out on something terribly important. He didn't like the feeling of rejection she gave him.

What the heck, he thought, I'm going to change that. Whatever it takes, I'll do it!

Having reaffirmed that resolution, Slade turned his attention to watching the Australian landscape unfold below them. The populous coastal region was very quickly left behind, and once over the mountains, the country changed dramatically. Vast rolling plains stretched endlessly, and the sheer distance between townships surprised him. The farther inland they went, the fewer signs of civilisation there were, and so much of the land seemed completely untamed by man. Signs of the long drought were everywhere, red earth bare of vegetation, scrubby trees more grey than green.

It was alien to any landscape Slade had seen before. Somehow it seemed imbued with an ancient timelessness and it was easy to imagine that it had not changed an iota since primitive man walked the earth. And primitive woman. He glanced at Rebecca. Perhaps that was the quality in her that tugged on something in his own soul. Untamed and elemental. Whatever it was, he wanted to explore it.

The pilot recalled his attention, pointing to a herd of kangaroos. "Pests to the graziers, particularly in times such as these. They've got to be culled to survive."

Slade watched them leap across the ground in a graceful flowing lope that held him fascinated. They were such a unique animal. "It seems such a shame," he protested.

"Nothing that can be done about it," the pilot said noncommittally. "It's a law of the land."

Slade repressed a feeling of horror. He hated killing of any kind. It seemed such a revocation of the very spirit of existence. Yet in a land like this, perhaps it did come down to the most primitive law of all, the law of survival. Was that why Rebecca Wilder was the way she was? Did that deep inner strength come from the continual fight to survive?

He looked at the kangaroos and wondered if the pilot was truly right when he said nothing could be done. Perhaps something could be done. Or was that thought the product of ingrained years of civilised living? He was a long, long way from New York. Did civilisation have any meaning at all here, in this country that Rebecca Wilder called home?

Slade was still musing on this idea when the pilot said, "There's a landmark coming up. That's Windy Drop-Down. And... Holy hell! What's going on down there?"

Slade saw it, too. A mob of cattle, the leaders standing up to their knees in water, the rest pressing forward, sprawling out behind, trying to get their drink. He saw one, two, three, four, five topple over and sink to their haunches. And it was not through weakness. They were being stopped dead by bullets!

Rebecca was suddenly between him and the pilot. She'd seen it, too. Slade felt a queasiness pass through his stomach. He knew without a doubt that these were his cattle, and they were infringing on her water rights. Even the horror of the killing going on could not outstrip the terrible sinking sensation that it was his fault. He couldn't bring himself to look at Rebecca.

"Pilot, get this plane down!" Her order was curt, imperative.

"It's not all that good a landing place."

"There's killing going on down there," she said tersely. "And it could get a lot worse before it gets better. I intend to stop it. Just get this plane down, pilot."

"Do as she says," Slade put in quickly, adding his support to Rebecca's command.

"Okay, lady. If that's what you want."

"And buzz them before you land."

"How low do you want me to go?"

"Clip their hair!"

"Right-oh!"

The pilot banked the plane and screamed towards the trouble area, levelling off only inches from the ground. Rebecca didn't even flinch. Without fear, Slade thought. She is completely without fear. Slade concentrated on giving nothing of his inner turmoil away. She's the one who hates flying, he thought. She should have been shaking in fear as they sped over the low contours of the ground, over a line of riflemen spread along the bank of the creek.

Slade saw more cattle being hit, their blood reddening the water. This was more terrible than he could conceive. But there was no sign of recoil from Rebecca Wilder.

"Put it down," she commanded in a steely voice.

"Where?"

"Close."

"Lady, far be it from me to advise you, but do you know what you're doing?"

"This is *my* land, pilot," she said fiercely. "And I will rule it!"

"Right! Fair enough! You'd better belt yourself in your seat then. I don't guarantee a smooth ride."

Slade gritted his teeth. Back in New York—was it only yesterday—he had idly thought he wanted an adventure. Landing a plane on rough ground and facing up to live bullets did not constitute his heart's desire. In fact, his heart was doing a lot of protesting. Along with his stomach. But a burst of adrenaline insisted that Rebecca Wilder was not about to find him wanting, not on her territory or any territory. It was a challenge to his manhood, and no way was Slade going to have his manhood diminished in the eyes of this woman.

The little plane shook as it bumped in its touchdown. It shook a lot more before it finally came to a halt. Slade heaved a very shaky sigh of relief and turned to Rebecca, who was already out of her seat.

"Open the door!" she called to the pilot.

It galvanized Slade into action. "Rebecca, you stay here. I'll go and sort this out."

"No way! I'm—"

He grabbed her arm to stop her. "You could get shot!"

The green eyes flashed scorn at him. "They wouldn't dare!" She tore her arm out of his grasp and leapt out of the plane.

He followed fast on her heels, driven by an overwhelming sense of urgency. He had to stop her, save her, protect her. "Rebecca!"

"You go and sort your lot out!" she threw at him contemptuously. "I'll deal with Emilio."

She sprinted off before he could begin to argue. She didn't even look back to see what he was doing.

I didn't intend to be a hero, Slade thought, but it looks like I'm going to have to be one. He could hear the desultory crack of the rifles and felt dazed with disbelief. But it *was* happening! He shook himself into action and started making for the creek, chasing after Rebecca Wilder.

The soil was sandy and heavy going. Rebecca was running lithely over it, he noticed. Sneakers on her feet. He was wearing the wrong darned shoes. He lifted his feet faster and moved into a better-paced jog.

He grinned. This was certifiable madness. If the executives Rebecca had faced in the boardroom could see him now. No wonder she had said they lived in a little eyrie high above the real world. If this was her world, New York would seem as unreal to her as this was to him!

I hope these gunslingers don't take me for a cow, he thought. The image of the man in the wheelchair flashed across his mind. What kind of courage could this girl inspire that you could risk ending up like that? Slade didn't know. All he knew was that he couldn't turn back, not even on that sobering thought. Wherever she went, he had to go. Or he'd never be able to look at himself in a mirror again!

He spotted the head of a man bobbing along above the bank of the creek. Slade quickened his pace. Rebecca still wasn't within his reach but he reckoned he could just about tackle her to the ground if some gun-happy cowhand started blasting his rifle in their direction. He almost hoped they would. He wanted to feel her body under his, to hold her, to stamp his domination on her.

The cattle, his cattle, were clearing away from the other side, panicked out of their thirst by the gunfire. He saw stockmen trying to round them up, bullwhips cracking around them. He started rehearsing the few choice words he was going to say to them when he got the chance!

Rebecca reached the edge of the bank, took up a belligerent stance and raised both arms in the air. "Cease your fire!" she yelled in a voice that roared command. "Emilio! Wherever you are, you'd better show yourself fast! This is my land! And don't let even one of your men forget it!"

"Hold your fire!" came the shout from farther along the creek.

Slade had just pulled to a halt at Rebecca's shoulder and those echoing words sounded pretty good to him. She set off striding towards the answering shout, completely ignoring him. Slade marched alongside her, determined on bolstering whatever argument she intended to put to Emilio, but uncomfortably aware that he would be regarded as the enemy until proven otherwise.

"You keep out of this, Slade!" Rebecca snapped at him as a group of men made their appearance some twenty yards away. "One word out of place and you're liable to get your head blown off. Just keep in the background until I'm ready to introduce you."

It made sense. He didn't like it, but reason insisted he should have some modicum of sense in this madness he had so recklessly embraced. He slackened his pace, letting her take the lead.

A tall, rangy man strode from the group to meet her. He swept off his hat as Rebecca took a confrontationist stand. His face was deeply tanned and weathered, his black hair liberally peppered with grey. Slade assessed his age at close to fifty but his lean hard physique wore none of the softness of civilisation. A tough adversary, Slade figured, feeling the fierce authority emanating from every inch of Emilio Dalvarez.

The hand holding the hat lifted to sweep accusingly at the other side of the creek. "They killed your grandmother!" he said in vehement tones.

"Killing cattle will not bring my grandmother back," Rebecca retorted just as vehemently. No backward step from her! Straight into counterattack! "It's the last thing she would have wanted, Emilio! And you know it!"

"They killed her!" he shouted in violent justification.

Slade's heart squeezed tight. Surely to God Emilio Dalvarez didn't mean murder. He couldn't mean...

"You think she would be dead if they hadn't kept pushing her beyond all reason?" Emilio argued passionately. "You think her heart would have given out if it wasn't stressed beyond bearing?" His other hand lifted with a clenched fist. "I tell you, Rebecca, they have to be stopped!"

Slade felt almost dizzy with relief. A heart attack had taken Rebecca's grandmother. He forgot Rebecca's instructions and stepped forward. "They will be stopped! I give you my word on that, Mr. Dalvarez. Within a week, the herd on Devil's Elbow will be reduced to whatever numbers both you and Miss Wilder consider reasonable."

Emilio Dalvarez looked him up and down in studied contempt. "Who is this man?" he demanded.

Rebecca shot Slade a furious look before addressing her fiery neighbour. "You know why I went to New York, Emilio. You know it was my grandmother's wish that our problems with Cordell Enterprises be settled peacefully. And that is precisely what is going to happen, Emilio. This man is Slade Cordell himself, come to make amends for all the trouble his organisation has caused."

Emilio stared at Slade with narrowed eyes, measuring him again and not particularly liking what he saw.

"I regret to be making your acquaintance under such strained circumstances, Mr. Dalvarez," Slade said, resolved to clear the air as much as he could. "But I can assure you that I do deliver what I promise."

Emilio's mouth curled in cynical dismissal as he stared at Rebecca. "You believe him after all that's happened?"

"He's here, Emilio," she pointed out strongly. "If Mr. Cordell hasn't done what he claims he intends to do within a week, I'll review the situation. Meanwhile, I've come home to bury my grandmother."

She paused.

Emilio looked discomfited. "A great loss to you, Rebecca. A great loss to all of us," he asserted gruffly.

"Call your men off, Emilio. Take them home."

He shot Slade a hostile glare but the aura of violence he had carried to this confrontation had been appreciatively dimmed. "In respect for your grandmother, I will do as you say, Rebecca."

He jammed his hat on, swung on his heel and marched towards his men. Rebecca muttered something indecipherable under her breath, then without even a cursory glance at Slade, she set off towards the plane. Slade quickly fell into step beside her.

"You said you'd send a message to your people," she bit out accusingly.

"I did! I don't know what went wrong, but I'm sure as heck going to find out," he assured her grimly.

Mistrust glittered in her eyes. "Your cattle should not have been there, Slade. It's your responsibility to get those carcasses out of my creek. And I want it done today."

"If I have to drag them out myself, it'll be done."

She said no more. She didn't have to say any more. Slade figured he was about as low as a rattlesnake in her estimation. So far all his words had been about as empty as a rattle, and it was well past time they gained a bit of substance. He had to make up the ground he had lost with her as fast as he could.

"Everything okay?" the pilot called to them as they neared the plane.

"It will be. When we get to Devil's Elbow," Slade replied darkly.

Rebecca said nothing until she was about to board the plane. Then she gave the pilot a tight little smile. "Thank you. That was a fine bit of flying."

The pilot grinned. "Oh, nothing like a bit of excitement to liven up a day! You're welcome, miss."

He was obviously as mad as everyone else out here, Slade thought. Maybe it was catching.

Rebecca nodded and climbed into the cabin. Slade resignedly strapped himself into the seat beside the pilot. No way was he going to win Brownie points by sitting next to Rebecca. She was one very tough lady. He wished he had known her grandmother.

It was a bumpy takeoff but Slade didn't care about bumps any more. What were a few bumps after what he had already been through? Oddly enough he was beginning to enjoy the feeling.

Whatever he made of the future, one thing was certain. He would make Rebecca Wilder concede to him if it was the last darned thing he did! The scorn in those glittering green eyes was going to change to something else before she saw the last of him!

CHAPTER SIX

FOR REBECCA, the next seven days seemed to pass by in a dream. She carried out all that was necessary with automatic authority, never once faltering in the role she had inherited on her grandmother's death. Everyone who lived and worked on Wildjanna was assured that nothing was going to change. The pattern of the past would continue into the future, a foundation on which to build. Only Rebecca knew how empty that future felt to her.

It was Sunday again. The mid-morning sun beat down relentlessly from a cloudless blue sky. The land was dry and parched, and what little grass remained was brown and brittle. The water in the creek was gradually creeping down to lower and lower levels. Would it last as long as they would need it?

Rebecca looked at the pitiless clear sky and knew the drought was not going to break today. She strolled slowly around the wide verandahs that skirted the whole homestead. Almost every room in the house opened onto them, but she had no desire to seek the cooler air closeted inside the wooden walls. As far as the eye could see in any direction, the land belonged to her, to Wildjanna. Normally she would have been filled with the pride of possession, the deep rich sense of belonging, but somehow that feeling evaded her.

She paused on the western verandah, looking out at the small family graveyard, trying to refire the purpose for which she had been born. In some strange way she felt detached from Wildjanna. It slowly came to her that this was caused by the aching sense of loneliness, the inner craving for a companion to love, and to be loved back. That unsatisfied yearning inside her was like a fog drifting between her and the solid realities of her life here.

Rebecca tried assuring herself that it was probably a weakness that time would eradicate. Losing Gran, facing up to the crushing of all hope with Paul... It had only been seven days, a week. A week in which Slade Cordell had certainly delivered what he had promised.

Rebecca's thoughts turned to the big Texan who had categorically proved he was as good as his word. He had laid all scepticism to rest from the moment he had first confronted the management at Devil's Elbow with their failure to carry out his direct order concerning the cattle. It was then discovered that, as a final act of revenge, Mr. Petrie had sabotaged the order sent from the head office in New York. Instead of "Keep all stock from watering at Wildjanna," the message had read, "Keep stock watering at Wildjanna."

Slade's ice-cold fury had been too awesome not to be believed, and the quiet steely authority that had characterised his leadership in the Manhattan boardroom had the men at Devil's Elbow shaking in their boots. He had demanded immediate action and there had been action aplenty at Devil's Elbow over the past seven days.

The carcasses of the dead cattle had been removed by tractors and buried by a bulldozer. From Monday there had been a steady stream of cattle trucks coming and going, shifting the excess stock to a glutted market. The price Slade received was abysmal, but he had sold without any regard for the cost to himself.

And Rebecca had to admire the way he had handled
Emilio Dalvarez. It had been a master stroke of diplomacy
to ask for Emilio's advice on station management, stock
levels and on the sinking of artesian bores to the water ba-
sin that lay deep beneath the Channel Country. The bores
were an expensive business, drilling through layers of rock,
and sometimes the subterranean water tapped contained too
many minerals to be used for watering stock, but Slade was
apparently intent on not sparing any expense in implement-
ing solutions to the problems caused by the drought.

Established as chief advisor, the Argentinian's pride had
been well and truly salved. He had even reported to Rebecca that Slade Cordell was a man of sense who saw what
had to be done and did it. Sanity at last prevailed.

Rebecca knew she should be relieved that the crisis was
over. And of course she was. Not only did it reduce the
problems caused by the drought to a manageable level, but
it meant Slade Cordell would soon be on his way back to
New York. And out of her life.

Better he go as soon as possible. He stirred needs and desires that he would never answer, certainly not in any permanent sense. The way he had stood by her side at her
grandmother's funeral, assuming the role of supporting
consort, looking after her... it was wrong. It should have
been Paul holding her arm, seeing that she had refreshments, finding a chair for her to sit down. It should have
been a man who truly cared about her, not one who only
wanted to get into bed with her.

That was what Slade wanted. He hadn't tried to hide it
from her. Every time she had met those compelling blue
eyes, she had felt it. He had somehow made her feel it, an
unwilling physical attraction that he would exploit if she
showed any response to it. But for the circumstances, he
might have acted a lot differently. As it was, he had been

sensitive enough to realise what an emotion-laden day it was, and he had taken his leave without pressing her for anything. She had not seen him since. Which was fine by her!

She didn't want to see him. Slade Cordell was no answer to her personal needs. More likely than not he was planning his return to New York right now. There was no point in even thinking about him.

She stepped off the verandah and walked to the small burial ground where two generations of her family had been laid to rest. The picket fence that protected it had been freshly painted, one of the first orders Rebecca had given on arriving home. She opened the gate and stepped inside, seeking some solace for her miserable discontent.

The graves were all marked by headstones except for Gran's. A temporary wooden cross stood at the head of the newly turned earth. It would soon be replaced by a more fitting memorial for the matriarch of the family—the matriarch of Wildjanna.

Rebecca knelt to pick up a handful of loose soil. She watched it trickle through her fingers. The sands of time moved relentlessly on. She was twenty-six years old. At that age Gran had already given birth to her first son.

Emilio Dalvarez's manner towards her at the funeral had set Rebecca's teeth on edge. He had been altogether too gallant. It was obvious that when he considered a decent interval had passed, he intended to offer himself as a husband and partner. She was a young woman, in need of his manly advice and protection.

Rebecca wanted a fourth generation, but not through Emilio Dalvarez. Yet to have a child of her own, a child to love... If he gave her that, would it be worth overlooking the rest? Everything within her recoiled from accepting Emilio. He would take over any child she bore him, fighting her to assert his own kind of upbringing. If it was a daughter, he would expect her to do woman's work. If it was a son, he would do his utmost to mould him into his own image. Either way, the chances were that the child would become more a Dalvarez than a Wilder. Or be torn by the conflict between both parents.

No, Rebecca knew in her heart that she had to find some other answer. If only she could find someone like Slade Cordell to stand by her side for the rest of her life, to give her the children she wanted for Wildjanna...

A shadow fell across her grandmother's grave. Rebecca looked up. Her heart skipped a beat as she recognised the man who made the picket fence seem like an insubstantial barrier. The dark blue eyes begged her tolerance.

"Please forgive the intrusion," Slade said quietly. "I called at the house. Mrs. Hartigan thought you should be wearing a hat out here. So I—" he held out the wide-brimmed Akubra that Milly had given him to deliver personally to Rebecca "—hope you don't mind."

She straightened up, an ironic little smile hovering on her lips as she stepped forward to take the hat. "Milly's been fussing over me all week," she explained. "It's her way of... coping with things."

He cleared his throat. "I came to see you. To invite you to carry out an inspection of Logan's, er, Devil's Elbow. I hope that what I've done will meet your expectations."

"I'll take your word for it, Slade," she said, more in apology for her former mistrust than in rejection of his offer. "I'm sure you've done everything that's necessary."

He looked disappointed, vexed by her dismissal. "I'm going home in a few days," he said flatly. "I don't have much choice. There are a lot of loose ends I've got to fix up in New York. And a lot of people depending on me making the right decision at the right time."

It was what she had expected. It was patently absurd for her to feel deflated by the news that he was actually going back to his life in New York. Yet somehow it made her feel even more lonely. Nevertheless, even though Slade had nursed an ulterior motive for coming to Australia with her, he had been more than generous in his actions and with his time, so she dredged up a smile and aimed it fairly at him.

"I wish to thank you for all the trouble you've taken to get things sorted out."

He stared at her smile as if dazed by it. He took a deep breath and dragged his eyes back to hers. "Rebecca." He said her name in a soft yearning throb that seemed to curl around her heart and squeeze it tight.

Strong animal magnetism, her mind screamed. That was all it was. And he *was* going, leaving her world and returning to his city life. There could never be anything between them. Words spilled off her tongue in pure defence against the turmoil he was evoking inside her.

"It was good of you to come halfway across the world... and be here at this time. The integrity you've shown...your kindness and diplomacy... I'm sorry for my manner towards you at the beginning. Meeting you, knowing you has been the one pleasant thing that's come out of this mess. You've honoured all your promises and I deeply appreciate the way you've done it."

Her gaze fluttered down to the open-necked V of his shirt, denying the naked desire in his eyes. His broad chest rose and fell under the thin cotton.

"Rebecca!" he rasped, frustration gravelling over something like desperation. Then in one long passionate outburst he swept restraint aside. "Rebecca, you are the most *tantalising* woman I've ever met. Things between us would have been so different if events hadn't happened as they have. I know this is the wrong time and the wrong place, and you probably still blame me for your grandmother's death, so I'm the wrong man as well as everything else, but I don't know what more I can say, what more I can do..." His breath hissed out in a long ragged sigh.

"I don't blame you for Gran's death, Slade," Rebecca said quietly. She forced her gaze up to meet his, anxious to stop what he was clearly going to say, flinching at the raw wanting that glittered down at her. "Things couldn't have been different. You're the wrong man anyway," she said bluntly. "So it's best if we simply say goodbye and get on with our own lives."

"Give us the chance to get to know each other," he argued.

His voice was soft but his eyes were determined. There was not going to be any avoiding of what was on his mind, what was pulsing from him...and reaching her in debilitating waves. Rebecca stiffened her spine. She might feel weak but there was no way she would act weak. Her mouth curled into a deliberate taunt.

"Desire, Slade. Is that what you mean?"

His eyes bored at her with demanding intensity. "It's been there from our first meeting, Rebecca. Rivetting, twisting, knotting sexual attraction. Call it desire if you like. But if you're honest, you'll admit it got to you, too."

Her chin lifted in angry pride. "All right. I admit you have a certain attraction for me. That changes nothing. I see no future in it. I'll never give in to it."

She turned away, wishing the subject had never been raised. It hurt. This whole scene hurt. She heard the gate creak. "No!" she cried, even as his hand fell on her shoulder.

"You're no frightened little wimp, Rebecca." He swung her around to face him, his eyes ablaze with purpose. "There's a steel in you that even I find daunting. And exciting. You don't run away from anything. When you want something, you go for it. And you want *me*. So don't evade the issue by talking about a future that neither of us can see right now.''

The sheer force of his challenge punched through Rebecca's sense of discretion. Shaken by the physical power of his closeness, she broke away from him, stepped back and vehemently swung an arm out to encompass Wildjanna.

''This is my future! These are the graves on which it is built. This is my heritage. And the heritage of my children. Where do you fit, Slade?''

''Don't rule me out, Rebecca. You judged me once before, remember? And you were wrong!''

She shook her head and deliberately moved to the head of her grandmother's grave. She lay her hand on the top of the wooden cross. ''You'll never be to me what Pa was to Gran. That goes beyond desire, Slade. It's the deepest commitment a man and woman can give to each other. A sharing of far more than bodies. I might have had that with Paul. Never with you.''

''Why Paul?'' Slade picked up instantly, demandingly, the challenge he projected in no way diminished. ''Why not me?''

Hot colour flared into her cheeks. Her eyes defied him and the strong sexuality he emitted. ''Because Paul Neilsen belonged here. He loved this land before...'' Tears blurred her eyes. She swallowed hard, forcing down the lump of desolation that choked her throat. ''You saw him at the airport. We were to be married...but he won't marry me now.''

Resentment welled up in her as Slade simply stood there in grim silence, absorbing her words without comment, so blatantly virile that it hurt unbearably.

"You're the first man I've felt anything for since Paul's accident. It's been a year since… It's a physical thing that's beyond my control," she bit out angrily. "But I wouldn't go to bed with you to slake some sexual frustration, Slade. I'd make love with you for only one purpose, and that purpose would be to have a child."

The words had simply spilled out of the turmoil that had been going through her mind. Whether or not it was a mistake to have voiced them, it was impossible to determine. Somehow Rebecca felt cleansed, as though the very act of getting everything out into the open wiped away the grounds for Slade to persist in his desire for a brief fling with her.

Slade Cordell's face could have been carved from marble, totally inscrutable. "That's why there can never be anything between us," she said with decisive finality. "That's why I'll always reject you. I want more than you're prepared to give me."

Slowly his expression changed. The muscles around his mouth tightened. His eyes glittered. "Why tell me this, Rebecca? Why didn't you just use me? Why spurn me physically, when with the slightest little encouragement, and without me being any the wiser, you could have got me to serve your purpose?" he asked, his voice deep with dangerous undercurrents.

She gave a harsh little laugh, needing to break the tension that flowed from him. Her eyes filled with bitter mockery aimed at both of them.

"Perhaps I'm not as ruthless as you, Slade. To use someone to fulfil a need, use them intimately… and walk away afterwards. Perhaps I hope I'll find someone who'll fulfil all my needs, and who'll stand at my side for the rest of my life. Not for just a day. Or a night."

His dark blue eyes seemed to pierce her heart. Then his gaze lifted and swept out over Wildjanna. He turned away and walked slowly to the other end of the small graveyard. He stood there, his back rigid, his head tilted up, silent and totally motionless for several long, nerve-tearing minutes.

Rebecca watched him with glazed eyes, unable to bring herself to do or say anything. What he was contemplating she had no idea. She could hardly believe she had said as much as she had. The words had been torn from her very soul, and they had probably wounded his male pride, yet the truth was the truth no matter how unpalatable it was to him and his desires.

Paul had forced her to see the truth seven days ago. It put a stop to futile dreaming. Slade Cordell should thank her for not wasting any more of his time. He might feel frustrated about not getting what he wanted, but that would soon pass when he went back to his life in New York.

He turned and began to walk to her, pausing every couple of steps to read the headstones on the graves; her little brother, mother, father, uncle and finally Pa, who had carved out a life that had meaning to him, who had founded a family that would always have solid roots in a solid world.

Desire to fulfill his own needs was all it was with Slade, Rebecca thought dully. Yet when he lifted his gaze, and his vivid blue eyes locked onto hers, it was not desire but determination that burned from them.

"You want a child," he stated in that quiet voice that sliced to the heart of any issue. "I presume that's why Paul Neilsen won't marry you. Because he can no longer give you one."

It wasn't true. But pride held Rebecca's tongue. Slade had seen her on her knees, begging Paul to marry her. It was too humiliating to let him know the truth of Paul's rejection. It was less galling for Slade to believe that the man to whom she had given her love and loyalty had considered her needs above his own.

He was waiting for a reply. She stared back steadily and said, "That's none of your business, Slade."

A look of derision flitted over his face. His disturbingly direct gaze dropped to her grandmother's grave, lifted to the top of the wooden cross where Rebecca's hand still rested, her fingers almost white from the tight grip she had on it. His face seemed to sharpen, a conflict of interests warring across it, but when he lifted his eyes to hers again, they held a hard, relentless gleam.

"Don't you ever get lonely, Rebecca?" he asked in a soft insidious drawl that wound around her brittle defences.

"Perhaps that's why I want a child," she replied tersely, unable to deny what he so clearly perceived.

"Exactly." He bit out the word, then started walking slowly towards her, continuing to speak in that soft Texas drawl, his eyes holding hers in challenge. "Doesn't it seem wasteful to you to turn me away when I'm right here on your doorstep? On your own admission you find me attractive enough to consider the possibility of having a child by me. So why not take this opportunity, Rebecca? Why not go for what you want?"

He halted a bare half-step away from her. One hand lifted to cup her cheek, his thumb lightly caressing her tilted chin. Rebecca was so mesmerised by his words that she didn't even think to evade his touch.

"What's to stop you now?" he taunted softly. "I'm available, willing and able. And you won't be ruthlessly using me. I'm offering. The only thing preventing you from having the marriage you want with Paul Neilsen is the unfortunate fact that he can't provide you with the fourth generation for Wildjanna. If you become pregnant by me, you can go to him again, can't you? You can have it all, Rebecca. A child, the man you love, the future you want. All you have to do is take me first."

She stared at him incredulously. He was offering to father a child, and then to make no claim on it whatsoever! She could have a child of his to keep as her own. A fourth generation for Wildjanna. A child that might take after him, strong and indomitable, a worthy heir to a line of pioneers.

Slade's logic was falsely based, but every instinct Rebecca had was screaming that life didn't work by logic, anyway. The temptation he offered kept worming its way through her mind. His child...her child. She could not wrench her eyes from the hypnotic challenge in his. She could feel her heart hammering wildly against her chest. Her mouth had gone completely dry. She knew she should somehow deny all he said, but she could not find the will to take that critical step away from him.

"There are turning points in our lives where we are given a choice," he continued persuasively. "From that choice you can either forge your own destiny or be a cipher to the will of others. So much of what can be achieved is in the timing. You can tell me to go...or ask me to stay. Make your choice, Rebecca."

The web of temptation he had woven so powerfully clung around Rebecca's mind, making any clear thought impossible. Except what he offered had to be wrong. His whole argument was centred on her wants, her needs, the fulfilment of her future. What about him?

She remembered her strong impression of him in his New York office. Not a man of impulse, but a man who calculated every move. The question that had hovered in her mind then at last found voice.

"What do you get out of it, Slade?" she accused more than asked, and was mortified to hear her voice shaking.

He smiled, a slow smile that churned her stomach into knots. "I get to have you, Rebecca." The desire was back, simmering in his eyes. "That's what I want," he added unnecessarily.

Rebecca once again felt a treacherous warmth spreading through her. How he could evoke this response in her she didn't understand. She hardly knew the man. She didn't love him. Couldn't love him. In some ways he was totally alien to her. Yet she couldn't quite bring herself to turn her back on what he was offering.

"Is that all you want, Slade? Just to have me? You won't mind walking away afterwards?" she asked, torn by the feeling that if she gave herself to him, it might not be all that easy to see him walk away from her. There was something irresistible about Slade Cordell, something that made her feel he made his mark on everything he touched. A permanent mark. She knew that if she gave in to him she would hurt for the rest of her life.

"I'll go when you want me to go," he stated unequivocally. "You have my word on that. I won't linger around if I'm not welcome."

What if she didn't want him to go? What if... But the situation forbade her to ask those questions. They were too cold, too calculating. *Just for once, think with your feelings, your emotions,* Rebecca urged herself. For however short a time it might be, he would fill the emptiness and she wouldn't be alone. And if he left her with a child, she would never be alone again. A child fathered by him...

Of course he would inevitably return to his life in New York. That was too obvious to question. He had a vast organisation to run, thousands of employees whose livelihoods were linked to his leadership. What he was offering her was a brief encounter that was supposed to satisfy both of them. There was no hope of him staying with her. No hope...

Perhaps he saw the uncertainties raging in her eyes. Perhaps he wasn't sure that the seduction of words would be enough. The hand that had been warmly curved around her cheek suddenly shifted, softly raking through the hair above her ear. There was a touch on her waist but she didn't have time to think about that. His head was bending towards hers. Rebecca raised a hand, which fluttered ineffectually against the broad chest that was moving closer, but she did nothing at all to evade the kiss. Her lips tingled sharply as his mouth brushed softly over hers, warm flesh against flesh.

It had been so long since Rebecca had been kissed that for the first few seconds, she submitted to the contact with almost clinical detachment. Then the tantalising caress changed to a slow sensual pressure that sent tiny waves of sensation rippling through her whole body. Rebecca wasn't conscious of dropping her hat so that she could lift both hands to his shoulders. It was an instinctive reaction to what was happening to her, what Slade was making happen with a seductive expertise that coaxed her lips into tremulously parting. She felt his tongue tease the tip of hers, then in one smooth sweep of his arm, he gathered her in against the pulsing heat and strength and power of his body.

An overwhelming awareness of his masculinity flooded through her. She wanted what he offered. The power of sexual attraction, so long denied, exploded into chaotic reality. She made a tiny sound of approval deep in her throat, and as if it was a sign that Slade had been waiting for, his tongue lashed over hers in movements that shocked her with their knowing intimacy, shocked and excited her in ways she had never before experienced, and desire was no longer a mental image or a disturbing feeling, but a tide of mounting sensation that was an intense physical need for fulfilment. The quick arousal of his body in response to hers gave

her a wild wanton pleasure and a thrill of power. He held her
hard against him as he moved his mouth to whisper in her
ear.

"Ask me to stay, Rebecca." The words slid seductively
across her mind while his tongue traced her ear, making her
tingle at the sheer eroticism of the caress. "Ask me to stay,"
he murmured.

She said nothing, and Slade held her more firmly, his
mouth meeting hers again and again, his warm breath fan-
ning the flames in her cheeks, his hands caressing and
moulding her closer to him, beguiling her more totally with
every kiss and touch.

Again he said, "Ask me to stay."

Rebecca dimly realised that this was the end of the road.
If she said no or remained silent any longer, he would take
himself away from her and go back to New York. The
choice had been offered. She had to make it.

CHAPTER SEVEN

REBECCA NEEDED what Slade offered her, needed it far more than he could ever know. For the moment, she was totally uncaring of where it might lead, as long as Slade stayed with her now.

"Yes," she conceded.

His hands stilled. She felt his chest expand. A long breath wavered through her hair. Slowly, very slowly, he eased himself back from her and lifted his hands to her face. Rebecca wasn't sure she wanted to open her eyes, to see what was written in his, but she had made her decision, given her word, and there was no evading any of the consequences.

She lifted her lashes, ready to meet a blaze of triumphant satisfaction, but the expression in the dark blue eyes was far more complex than that—an oddly poignant mixture of relief and appeal and a deep wanting that was yet to be satisfied.

"Let me take you away where we can be alone together," he said huskily. "And let it be for only you and me, Rebecca. Babies are for the future, not the here and now. There's so little time. I'll delay going back to New York as long as possible, but it can only be a week at most. You could leave Wildjanna for a week, couldn't you? Everything's running smoothly. Just a week, Rebecca. Just for us. Because of what we can be together."

Somehow his argument sounded twisted up, but as Rebecca took in the ramifications of what she was about to do, she realised it would be better if they did go away. Milly would probably be scandalised if they remained at the homestead, and Slade's staying with her—or her with him—would inevitably give rise to the kind of speculation she didn't want to answer. Not yet.

If she became pregnant there would inevitably be talk to contend with, but she would face that when and if it happened. And finally, since this brief encounter was all she would have of Slade Cordell, she didn't want the time wasted on anything else.

"Where?" she asked.

His smile made Rebecca feel distinctly light-headed. "We hold some real estate on a place called Forty-Mile Beach. It's within easy driving distance from Brisbane. There's a cottage we can use. Completely private. No close neighbours. It sounds like the kind of place I want to be with you."

It posed no problems as far as Rebecca was concerned. She had a weird sense of unreality about the seeming casualness of what she had agreed to. Yet her inner acceptance that there was no turning back from it was strangely beyond question.

"That's fine," she said cautiously, aware that she shouldn't allow Slade to make all the rules. She had seen his dominant personality at work and could not deny its power on herself. She could not afford to fall victim to it in any lasting sense. A week out of her life. Then she was on her own again.

He stroked her cheeks as though she was as delicate and precious as porcelain china. "I'll look after you the best I can, Rebecca."

It would be so easy to become putty in his hands, Rebecca thought. It was an effort to produce a dry little smile. "I don't need looking after, Slade. What I'm doing is dangerous...for me. I figure you're about as deadly as any man can get. I don't want to pay too much for the pleasure of knowing you."

His face tightened into serious concern. "You won't get hurt, Rebecca, I promise you. I will look after you... And you're not to even think of having a baby...yet. Just give us time, Rebecca, so that we can both assess where we are and where we're going. You need to consider more deeply this matter of having a child."

An anxious note crept into his voice as he rushed on. "It's not easy being a single parent. A lot of people do it now, I know, but I feel there's got to be a better way than that. Whatever you can give a child at Wildjanna, and I admit there are natural advantages here, there will still be problems. Single parents have twice as much to do, twice the normal responsibilities..."

Single parent? Why was he suddenly assuming that outcome when he had argued she could use his child to get Paul to change his mind about marrying her? Not that she would...or could. But Slade certainly seemed to be backtracking, leaving Paul right out of her future.

"That choice is mine, Slade," Rebecca cut in, impatient with such unexpected scruples, which ran completely counter to the offer he had made. In any event, whether she had a baby or not was her decision and she would work out her problems her own way.

Slade took a deep breath, then spoke slowly, as though gingerly feeling his way. "We can only be together for a week this time, Rebecca, but I'll be back. I haven't finished with Devil's Elbow. There are things I want to do here. Which I *will* do as soon as I can make the organisational changes I need to make in New York. When I return—it will be in a few months—if you've really thought it all through and still want to have our child, we'll do it together."

A treacherous thrill raced through Rebecca, chasing the thought that this week would not be all she would ever have of Slade Cordell, and perhaps a much deeper relationship would become possible.

His hands slid down to grasp her arms and he spoke with urgent intensity. "Promise me, Rebecca, that you will leave the decision until then."

Another thought slid into her mind—a cold heart-twisting thought—what if he never came back?

In the four years Cordell Enterprises had owned Devil's Elbow, Slade had not had enough personal interest in it to even pay the vast property a flying visit. She couldn't imagine this past week had changed that attitude. It was quite plain now that he had come here because of her, and once his desire for her was appeased, it was far more likely that he would become submerged in his other interests again. It would be stupid to fool herself into believing he would ever change his life for her . . . or for the child he might father.

A gentle squeeze on her arm heightened his already strong physical claim on her. "You won't come back to New York with me, will you? You won't leave what you have here to be with me?"

A lifetime in that city, one of the biggest cities in the world? Rebecca's recoil from the idea was instantaneous and obvious.

Slade's mouth twisted in self-mockery. "No, I thought not."

She could not change her life, either. That was the reality. No matter what Slade made her feel—what he felt—after this week they would inevitably part to follow their own destinies.

"But I will return, Rebecca," Slade said softly, reminding her once again of his uncanny ability to pick up on her thoughts. "Don't doubt that."

She forced a smile. "One step at a time, Slade. I might change my mind about a lot of things by the end of our week together. As to when you return here, no doubt we'll both have had time to think more, and be sure of what we want."

Relief and satisfaction spread into his responding smile. "It will be a good week, Rebecca," he declared confidently, accepting her words as the promise he had demanded of her.

They were no such thing.

Going with him now was the first step. Rebecca was planning a great many more steps as she led him to the house.

Slade Cordell had already served one vital purpose. He had cast off the fog that had been drifting around her mind since Gran had died. Her life had meaning again, and her future path was suddenly very clear.

There was the children's project that she and Gran had discussed so often. That would most certainly become a reality, she silently promised her grandmother. And she would start on the new dam, which would become the lake they had envisaged. That would have to be done before the drought broke. The genetic breeding program could wait a while, but there was much to be accomplished before she gave birth to a child, the child that Slade Cordell had offered her, the child she would have if the law of nature followed its inevitable course.

Rebecca now knew where she was heading and what she had to do.

The trip to Forty-Mile Beach was organised with what Rebecca was coming to recognise as Slade Cordell's forceful efficiency. A few calls made from Wildjanna and everything was set in motion. Her own arrangements were relatively simple. She told Milly she was going to Brisbane with Slade to settle some business, left instructions for her top station hand, packed a bag with the clothes she would need and made her departure. A plane was waiting at Devil's Elbow by the time they arrived there. A car was waiting at Brisbane Airport to take them the rest of the way.

It was early evening by the time they reached the cottage, a typical Queenslander structure built of clapboard with an iron roof and verandahs running all around it. Rebecca had no idea when it had come into the possession of Cordell Enterprises, but both the white-painted cottage and the grounds around it were well maintained.

A high hedge of hibiscus trees provided privacy from any passersby, except from the beach front. Clumps of palm trees added their tropical touch, and the sweet scent of frangipani trees in full bloom wafted on the air. A rather patchy but neatly cut lawn spread to the white sand that stretched around the coastline for as far as the eye could see in either direction.

The interior of the cottage was designed for casual living. The kitchen, dining and lounging areas were arranged in an open plan, taking full advantage of the beach view provided by a wall of glass doors. There was a large bathroom between two bedrooms. Slade carried their bags into the more spacious bedroom facing the sea. Rebecca noticed that the bed had been made up with fresh linen and clean towels had been laid out. The kitchen had also been fully provisioned, although to save the bother of cooking a meal tonight, they had stopped along the way to buy fried chicken and salads.

As a lovers' hideaway, the whole place could not have been more ideal, but now they were here, Rebecca felt intensely awkward about the situation. Throughout the whole trip Slade had kept plying her with questions about her life, her family history, the various difficulties that had been overcome in establishing Wildjanna. His avid interest in knowing all she would tell him had not left her much time to think about how she would feel once they were alone like this. With Paul, nothing had ever really been calculated or planned. Lovemaking had been a natural progression of their feelings for each other. She simply did not know how to act with Slade. He was almost a stranger!

Afraid that he would perceive her inner tension, and inwardly cringing from appearing gauche to this sophisticated man of the world, Rebecca used the pretence of viewing everything there was to see before unpacking. She strolled out through the living room, opened one of the glass doors, crossed the wide verandah and leaned on the railing, ostensibly to breathe in the fresh invigorating smell of the ocean.

Part of her mind accused her of utter madness for making this choice. She was going to be hurt. It was inevitable. Because she did want more from Slade than he could or would ever give her. Another part argued that she had made the only pragmatic choice.

Her social world was very limited. She might never meet anyone she wanted to share her life with. The only man she had been attracted to since Paul was Slade. At least she would have a child, the child of a man she would have accepted as a mate if he had been born to her world.

She heard Slade step out onto the verandah. Rebecca hoped she looked relaxed as he joined her at the railing. She was intensely aware of him standing beside her, so aware that her skin prickled at his nearness and her pulse quickened to a wildly ragged tempo.

"There are very few places left in the world where one can enjoy something like this," he commented appreciatively. "There are no beaches, even in Hawaii, that could match what we have here. This has to be the best I've ever seen. To have an unpolluted seacoast that's not surrounded by high-rises and cluttered with people, just unspoiled nature at its best..."

Rebecca slid him an ironic smile. "I guess it's not going to stay that way. Your company wouldn't have bought this property for the purpose of conservation."

"No. I dare say it didn't. But now that I've seen it, well, I like it the way it is. It would be a shame to spoil it in any way at all. I'll keep that in mind when I do an investigation of all Dan Petrie's dealings." His brow creased in concern as he searched her eyes intently. "If you don't like it here, Rebecca, we can move somewhere else. Anywhere. Any time."

"It's fine, Slade. Truly!" she asserted, surprised that he should doubt her appreciation of the location.

He smiled his relief. "I just want you to be happy with me. If there's anything—"

"I know. You'll wave your magic wand and it will be done," she mocked lightly.

"It's not quite that simple!"

On that sighed comment, he turned her towards him, gently drawing her into his embrace. She could not restrain an involuntary shiver as his hand stroked down her back. Whether it was from apprehension or excitement she wasn't sure. It was difficult to think straight with Slade holding her close to him. She wanted, needed him to kiss her again, to make her forget that she didn't really know him or love him. His mouth brushed warmly over her temples and she tilted her face to his, but he did no more than meet her eyes with a look that was strained with repressed desire.

"I'm not going to rush you into bed, Rebecca," he said softly. "I meant what I said about getting to know each other. That's as important to me—more so—than any other satisfaction might be. There's no hurry. You can take your time. Nothing will happen until you're ready."

She stared at him, confused by a sense of disappointment and surprise at his sensitivity. She had thought him calculating and ruthless, yet he had shown tactful consideration towards her on the trip home from New York. As he was doing now. As he had done on the day of her grandmother's funeral. She decided that nothing about Slade Cordell could be taken for granted. He was indeed a very complex man, not easy to read at all.

"You said what you wanted was to have me, Slade," she reminded him questioningly.

"I will. When you're ready."

"I'm ready. As ready as I'm ever going to be," she insisted, willing her voice to remain perfectly steady and holding his gaze without the slightest flinch. The truth was she didn't want to get to know Slade Cordell too deeply. She was quite sure it was better not to. When it came time for the parting of the ways . . .

"You have no fear of anything, have you?" he said in a wondering, bemused tone of voice, and the admiration in his eyes emboldened her to take the next step.

She reached up and slid her hands over his powerful shoulders, around his neck. "You're not exactly a coward yourself, Slade." A wild streak of pride made her add, "I'm going to make certain this is as big an adventure for you as it is for me."

The sibilant expulsion of his breath fanned the hair at her temples. She felt the knot of tension in his body. Then he was crushing her to him, swinging her off her feet, moving with urgent purpose to the bedroom. He came to an abrupt halt at the foot of the bed, his chest heaving as he slowly set Rebecca on her feet. His face clearly bore the conflict of needs churning through his mind.

"Rebecca, are you organised for this?" he rasped. "Do you want me to take care of . . ."

"I'm organised," she assured him quickly, letting him interpret that any way he liked. She spun away from him before he asked any more questions, pulling her shirt over her head as she walked towards a chair near the windows on the other side of the bed, hoping that the action would distract him from thinking any more about contraception.

It was clear to her that it wouldn't sit easily on Slade's conscience to return to his own life if he left her carrying his child. He did not want the responsibility of any consequences from what he desired of her. He wanted to walk free, and she would let him, but she was not about to be cheated of the choice he had given her. She *was* organised for that choice. Slade might or might not come back to Devil's Elbow. There was no guarantee that he would still desire her if he did. She had this week, and it was all she could really count on.

With her mind feverishly justifying her actions, Rebecca stripped herself completely naked. She tossed each garment on the chair with a deliberate abandonment that denied any nervousness over what she was doing. Only when she had nothing else to remove did she pause to work up courage for the next step. She had to turn around and she didn't know what Slade was doing, what he was thinking. She had never stood naked in front of a man before, not even Paul.

But this was different, she argued to herself. What was about to take place with Slade was an act of nature, not of passion. It was a continuation of the life cycle natural to all living creatures since time began.

Even as Rebecca told herself that, her hands instinctively lifted to undo the hair clip at the nape of her neck. It joined the pile of clothes on the chair. She used her fingers to rake out the thick curtain of her long black hair, then only just resisted the impulse to pull it forward over her breasts. That would be a sign of weakness. She had made her choice.

She steeled herself with pride and purpose and turned to face the man she had chosen to be the father of her child, the man who would give her the fourth generation for Wild-janna.

CHAPTER EIGHT

SLADE HAD NOT MOVED. He still stood, as though struck to stone, precisely where she had left him. He was staring at her with an expression of dazed incredulity. If Rebecca didn't know better she'd have thought he had never seen a woman naked before.

She had no idea of how she looked to him. She thought her body was as feminine as most although she carried no excess flesh. Paul had once said she had perfect breasts, full and firm and beautifully shaped just for him. But that was lovers' talk. Her waist was naturally trim, emphasising the womanly curve of her hips. Her long legs were probably more muscular than those of women who led more sedentary lives, but they suited her well enough. She began to worry if she had turned Slade off by acting on her own instead of letting him take the initiative.

"Is something wrong?" she asked.

"No." The word came out huskily. He shook his head as though needing to clear it. She saw his throat work in a convulsive swallow. Even so, his next words sounded gravelly. "I've never met a woman like you before. No one remotely like you. Just...don't move, Rebecca. I want to look at you. I want to hold this image of you in my mind forever because I'll never see its like again."

His words, the admiring way he said them, sent a rush of prickling heat over her skin. "How long am I to stand before you like this before you're ready?" she mocked. He was making her too conscious of her nakedness, and she hadn't come with him simply to be looked at.

His mouth curved into a bemused little smile as he slowly lifted his hands to begin unbuttoning his shirt. "You don't even realise how unique, how magnificent you are. I don't know what it is... What draws me so strongly... Perhaps that wild unreachable quality about you. All I know at this moment is that you make me feel privileged just to look at you. That may sound crazy to you...."

He took off his shirt, and Rebecca was instantly distracted by the strong maleness of his powerful physique—the breadth of his shoulders, the impressive delineation of muscles that had certainly never suffered from his supposedly sedentary occupation. He had the look of a formidable athlete in top condition, and Rebecca couldn't help wondering how he managed to stay so fit. Suddenly it didn't seem at all crazy to simply want to look at a person. She wanted to look at him.

"Whatever the reason—" his hands moved to unzip his jeans "—this is not something I want to hurry over."

She had given him time to think, Rebecca realised. The desire that had surged through him on the verandah was now under control, forged to his will. She had a few moments of panic as she wondered what he meant to do with her. But the end was the same, she hastily reassured herself. The means didn't matter.

"I want you, Rebecca," he said softly.

She wrenched her gaze up to meet his, her heart fluttering wildly at the thought of their coming together. She remembered how it had been with Paul and felt a painful stab of disloyalty to the love they had shared. But Paul had betrayed that love. Not she. And she couldn't deny the surge of arousal in her own body as Slade began walking towards her.

"I want more than a simple meeting of flesh with flesh," he said, his voice husky with a yearning that knotted her stomach. "I want to reach that unreachable part of you that keeps its own counsel. I want to know all the inner secrets of your soul. I want the whole essence of you, Rebecca Wilder, not just the substance." He stroked feather-light fingertips from her throat to the deep valley between her breasts. "I want to touch... more than your skin."

He wanted too much, much too much! Every self-protective instinct Rebecca had was shrieking in protest at the surrender he wanted from her. She couldn't give it to him. She couldn't let him take that much from her. It would make her too vulnerable to him, and when he went away...

Rebecca didn't stop to reason it out. All she knew was that what Slade intended was dangerous to her and she had to take the initiative of this act of intimacy away from him before he entwined her too deeply into his needs. She reached out, provocatively sliding her hands down his tautly muscled thighs.

"Don't make me wait, Slade," she said invitingly, her eyes open mirrors of her need for him. She moved, bringing herself into contact with the potent thrust of his body, the tips of her breasts brushing against his chest.

She felt the uncontrollable tremor that ran through him, knew he was strained to the limit of his will power. "Kiss me," she asked, needing to be submerged in the mindless passion he had evoked in her before.

He groaned her name in half protest at her impatience, but the sound was stifled as his mouth crashed onto hers. There was no persuasive sensuality in the driving force of his passion to possess, and completely reckless in her desire to finish what had been started, Rebecca responded with an uninhibited wildness that she had not known herself capable of.

What followed was a savage kind of madness, like some primitive battle for supremacy that knew no boundaries. Slade's hands raked down her back, closed around the curved firmness of her buttocks and lifted her into more intimate pressure with his sexuality. Rebecca wound her legs around his thighs, enticing him to satisfy both of them. He swung around, tore his mouth from hers and strode for the bed, kneeling on it, kneeling over her as he laid her head on the pillows.

"No!" he breathed hoarsely, his eyes glittering into hers. "You won't have your way with me, Rebecca! I'll have more than that!"

He wrenched her hands from around his neck and pinned them above her head, silencing any protest she might have made with another plundering kiss, which she returned with all the violence of rebellion against his will. She used her feet to stroke the sensitive hollows at the backs of his knees. She arched her body to his, using all her feminine sexuality to deny him any control at all.

He was so strong, she had to be strong, too, as wilful as he was. Yet when he pushed himself down her body and his mouth closed over the sensitised peak of her breast, drawing on it with exquisite delicacy, she could not stop herself from crying out at the sweet agony-pleasure that pierced through her. Only then did he release her, freeing his hands to caress her into convulsive shivers of mindless pleasure.

And Rebecca gave up trying to fight him, trying to fight what he was doing to her. Her body seemed almost like an alien thing to her, producing reactions and responses and revelling in incredible waves of sensation, which drowned any coherent thought at all. Her arms felt heavy and drained of all strength. Her thighs quivered with uncontrollable excitement. She did not even know that her hands clutched Slade's head as he wrought this wild chaos inside her. She did not hear herself plead for the fulfilment of the craving that had built to an intolerable peak of expectancy.

But she saw his face when he moved to answer her need and knew that he had been caught up in the same sensual storm that raged through her. His eyes glittered with a feverish light. A harsh guttural sound of unbearable wanting broke from his lips as he drove himself deep within her. Rebecca arched up in a convulsive paroxysm of intense pleasure. His arms wrapped around her, clasping her body to his, imprinting the apocalyptic moment of absolute intimacy to the very depths of her soul.

He murmured soft comforting words that drifted through her mind without making any real sense. Then slowly he built a rhythm of spiralling delight, which was so intense that Rebecca felt she would die from it. Yet her body wantonly adapted to every exquisite movement he made, voluptuously inciting the eventual shattering of any last thread of control he held. The erotic pulse of his possession quickened into a fierce plunging need that swept them both to an explosive climax. And then there was only a sweet flooding warmth, a mindless desire to cling to each other as their inner lives merged and ebbed, sealing a union that took them far beyond any sense of self.

It was a long time before Rebecca even began to think. She felt so relaxed and drowsy and the languorous pleasure of simply lying in Slade's arms was an experience she wanted to savour. She liked the feeling of her naked flesh against his. She hadn't realised how deliciously sensual it could be to lie with a man like this without any barrier of clothing between them, and Slade certainly had a magnificent male body. He somehow made her feel more conscious of her own differing sexuality than she had ever been in her life.

She and Paul had never shared the erotic heights of lovemaking that Slade had brought her to. It didn't seem right that the most intense physical pleasure could be attained without love. But there was a vast difference between emotional satisfaction and sexual satisfaction. Slade was certainly an expert lover, but all he would ever give her was an experience . . . and she hoped a child would come of it.

A bleakness swept through her at the thought that this week would probably be all she would ever have of even this kind of loving. As for the other kind, she knew that what she had once had with Paul was over. It hadn't really been what she had imagined it to be—the lifelong commitment that nothing but death could break.

Strange, the desolation she had felt over that revelation was gone now. In making this momentous choice, had she put the lingering emotionalism of her relationship with Paul to rest?

Somehow that didn't seem right, either. She had loved Paul. . . . Or had she? Maybe she had simply clung to him because he was the only man who had ever offered her the chance of having the kind of relationship that Gran and Pa had shared. And after the accident, impossible to consider anything else; so she had clung on blindly, even though she should have seen Paul didn't want her kind of life any more. Perhaps she had despaired of there ever being anyone else for her . . . that Paul was the one chance. A mate. A partner. Someone to love her as Pa had loved Gran.

The actual truth was she felt a deeper tug of attraction towards Slade than she had ever felt towards Paul. As many times as she had told herself there was no future in it—and there wasn't—there was no denying Slade Cordell touched many deep chords in her. Deeper than Rebecca cared to examine.

Tears filled her eyes. What had to be done with Slade was done for now. She shouldn't be luxuriating in intimate togetherness that would make her long for it when it was gone.

She had to keep things in perspective or she would end up in a wretched mass of confusion. She had never envisaged herself doing anything like this—giving herself to a man who offered her nothing of himself except his body.

She pushed herself away from him. The togetherness was a lie. They were destined to go separate ways. She had to keep that in the forefront of her mind as a defence against wanting more than she could have.

"Rebecca . . ."

Slade rolled onto his side, checking any evasion from him too fast for her to blink away the tears that clung to her thick lashes, and his keen blue eyes didn't miss them. The look of pained tenderness that crossed his face forced her to deny any real distress.

"Are you always that good with every woman, Slade?" she asked, a hard brittle edge to her voice.

His mouth twisted into a self-deprecating grimace. "Not good enough apparently," he murmured. Very gently he smeared the spill of moisture from the corners of her eyes. "You're thinking of him, aren't you?"

Slade was wrong about what was running through her mind. Although not entirely wrong. She had been thinking of Paul, and the general accuracy of Slade's perception stirred Rebecca to question it.

"Am I so easy for you to read?" she asked.

"No. But if you love him, it's only natural that you should be thinking of him now," he answered with an understanding that shook Rebecca even further.

She stared at him searchingly, yet found no resentment in his eyes. "You don't mind, Slade?"

"Yes. I mind," he said with a soft little half-smile. "I'd be less than honest if I didn't admit I'd prefer you to be thinking of me—us—and what we can have together."

She reached up and touched his cheek, deeply moved by his frank admission and driven to make an equally frank acknowledgement of what they had just shared. "I've never felt what you made me feel. I'll always be grateful to you for giving me that, Slade. Whatever else happens, at least I've known what it can be like. What it feels like to be...loved."

"Rebecca—" He sighed and shook his head. "Believe me, that was not like anything I've ever experienced either. You are what you are, and you answer something in me that I've never really known before. I guess that doesn't make much sense to you, and it doesn't really matter..."

It made sense. More than she would ever let Slade know, since it didn't really matter to him.

"In one way I feel very envious of Paul Neilsen," he mused wryly, "but not enough to change places with him. At least I have this much of you, and I imagine he would envy me, if he knew."

She flinched away from that thought. She wasn't at all sure that Paul would envy Slade at all. Not now.

"We all have to face realities, Rebecca," he said quietly. "You do that with an implacability that is completely beyond most people. So tell me about Paul Neilsen. Tell me what happened that resulted in his being tied to a wheelchair."

Perhaps it was the strange intimacy of the moment that drew her into recalling that terrible day. Or perhaps it was the compassionate understanding that flowed from Slade. In an odd way it was almost a release of her own deep guilt to talk about it. It also helped to deflect her growing awareness of what it might mean to her when Slade left to take up his real life. It was easier to recall the past than to contemplate the future.

"Paul flew helicopters. He loved their mobility—" her voice cracked a little as she thought of how much Paul's freedom of mobility was curtailed now...it was so wrong, so unfair "—and he loved the outback," she said with all her own deep passion for it. "He loved the space, the vastness of the country, the sense of being part of something bigger than more civilised forms of life. We always contracted him to help do the mustering from the outer boundaries on Wildjanna. He was especially skilled at that and enjoyed the challenge of getting the cattle on the move in the right direction...."

Her eyes dilated with the pain of remembrance as she continued. "I was at the mustering camp with Gran. I don't know to this day what spooked the herd of cattle Paul was driving in, but they started stampeding towards the camp. Paul saw the danger to us. He flew ahead of the leaders and brought the helicopter down in a low swoop to turn them away from us. He flew too low. The rotors clipped a tree and the helicopter spun out of control. It crashed into another tree. Paul's back was broken, his legs crushed, and—" she closed her eyes over another rush of tears.

"So he risked his own life to save you and your grandmother," Slade murmured.

She opened her eyes in bleak acknowledgement. "Yes. And the cost to him..."

Slade placed a silencing finger on her trembling lips, and the dark blue eyes bored sharply into hers. "It wasn't your fault, Rebecca. It was his choice. And life moves on in its own inexorable way. What does Paul do now?"

She swallowed the lump of emotion blocking her throat. Slade was right. She knew he was. But sometimes that didn't help to wipe out the misery that lay deep in her heart over what could never be changed.

"He was always good with machines. He's working on some computer technology for boats and planes. He's turned it into a business, which is going very well," she stated flatly. "He's...very successful."

Slade nodded. "A strong resourceful man. He couldn't be anything else."

"Why do you say that?"

"Rebecca..." He gave her a slow knowing smile. "They say that opposites attract, but it's far more common like attracts like. His strengths are your strengths. And you may not want to recognise it yet, but that's part of why we're attracted to each other. It's not completely physical. Not all of it."

She frowned, knowing it was not all of it, yet conscious they were poles apart in the way they viewed life. Just to show how obvious this was, she made a point of it.

"How old are you, Slade?"

"Thirty-six."

"I don't understand why it doesn't matter to you to have a woman you love at your side," she said questioningly.

His face hardened and a weary cynicism settled in his eyes. "I guess marriage can work for some people. It's most unlikely that it would ever work for me. That's the reality, and I'd be a fool not to face it, much as I might prefer it to be different."

"Why won't it work for you?" she persisted. "If you truly love someone—"

"What is love?" he cut in, his eyes sharply probing hers. "You say it's sharing everything. How do you get to sharing everything? I've had plenty of mutual attractions...but none stuck beyond the initial novelty."

Was that what she was to him? A novelty? Rebecca quickly crushed the wave of hurt, forcing herself to be ruthlessly practical. It didn't matter. She knew—she wasn't depending on it—that Slade Cordell wouldn't be part of her future. Only his child. If she conceived.

"Why didn't they stick?" she asked.

He expelled a heavy sigh and spoke in his slow Texas drawl. "One of the penalties of being what I am is that many people see me only as a figurehead of power. Economic power, corporate power, political power, power over people's lives, take your pick. It's true. I have all that. And it's been a large part of my attraction for every woman I've ever had. After a while I realise they're never going to see beyond that to the me I know. The me inside my head. The me that matters to me."

"Do you give them a chance to know the inner you?" Rebecca asked curiously.

His mouth curled in self-mockery. "Maybe not. Maybe no one has cared enough to try. After all, I have so much else. Why search for the soul inside a man when his bank account is as large as mine?"

"I don't care about your bank account," Rebecca said defensively, bridling against his cynicism.

"I know," he said softly. His eyes momentarily darkened with a hungry yearning. Then his mouth twisted in dry irony. "Nor are you out to use me in the usual way."

Rebecca realised, with a nasty jolt, that she was using him as a stepping stone to her own future. The discomfiting thought didn't sit well on her conscience. Slade was just as human as anyone else. He had feelings to be hurt, and she sensed that he covered a hurting emptiness with his cynicism. Yet this week ... It was not as if he was seriously involved with her. He was only after some *novelty*, wasn't he?

"You offered, Slade. If you hadn't offered I wouldn't be *using* you at all. You wanted me to use you so that you could have this," she said testily, needing to confirm that she wasn't mistaken about his motives for wanting her with him.

She saw uncertainty flicker in his eyes, a flash of vulnerability that twisted her heart, then a quick firming of resolution. "Yes. I wanted this with you. Whatever I can have with you."

His reply relieved her mind to some extent, yet she felt a strong empathy for the inner loneliness it implied. She suddenly wanted, needed to give him as much as she could during their short time together. At least it would be some return for what he would give her, albeit without his knowledge. That was only fair!

"Slade..." She moved her hand to curl around his neck and draw him down to her. "Please kiss me again," she invited, her eyes warmer than they had ever been for him before.

It sparked a responding warmth in his eyes that quickly kindled into a blaze of desire. "You know I won't stop at kissing, Rebecca," he warned.

"I know." She smiled. "I don't want you to stop. I'd like you to tell me how I can give you more pleasure this time. I want to make this good for you, Slade."

His swift intake of breath was intensely expressive of the impact of her words. He hadn't expected to hear that from her after her earlier rejection of their intimacy. But she would make it up to him, Rebecca vowed to herself.

He wrenched his gaze from hers, ran it slowly down the outstretched nakedness of her body, then just as slowly returned it to her eyes. "You have one of the most provocatively sexy bodies I've ever seen, yet it's more the thought of you that excites me, Rebecca. If you didn't touch me at all, I'd still want you. Whatever pleases you will please me," he said, his voice husky with anticipation as he bent his head to hers.

There was no wild tempest of passion this time, yet in a totally different way their lovemaking was a much deeper sharing of themselves. There was a tenderness, a caring that had been missing before, a more conscious intimacy that was given and received with a fresh appreciation of each other. And when they finally lay entwined in the peaceful aftermath of contented fulfilment, Rebecca made no move to separate herself from him. It felt right and good to stay nestled in the warm security of Slade's embrace. She didn't feel alone.

CHAPTER NINE

FOR REBECCA it was a strange week. In one sense it was almost a fantasy come true. It bore no relation to what she thought of as her real life. There was no work to be done apart from a few household chores, which Slade shared with her. There were no responsibilities, nothing to plan except what pleasure to indulge themselves in next.

Each day was a hedonistic delight. They ate makeshift meals, swam in the crystal-clear waters of a brilliant turquoise sea, offered their bodies to the sun on the warm white sand and made love in so many erotic and gratifying ways that every experience made the next even more addictive.

She supposed it could be likened to a honeymoon, except for the sharp awareness that once it was over, it was over. There had been so little between herself and Slade beforehand, and there was certainly no promise of continuance after the week ended, yet they forged a kind of intimacy many newly married couples might have envied.

Rebecca wasn't even sure how it evolved, nor did she feel inclined to question it too deeply. She liked Slade's company. She found that his shrewd perception of people and understanding of them was far beyond her own experience. He opened up his world to her, and although the revelations on how he managed his business empire were fascinating in an objective sense, they made Rebecca more convinced she would never want to be part of such a life.

Nevertheless that didn't stop her from respecting Slade's abilities, nor his command of all that had been achieved. He was a remarkable person, and Rebecca admired his strength of purpose and the talent and tenacity that had earned him his position as head of Cordell Enterprises. It had been no family sinecure. It was his place by right of his own dynamic intelligence and personality—a force to be reckoned with!

"Was it always your ambition to head the company your father founded?" she asked, wondering if it ran in his blood as Wildjanna ran in hers.

They were lying on the beach, Rebecca propped up on her elbow to watch Slade as he talked. She liked watching him, the lithe confident way he moved, seemingly never unsure of himself or what he was doing, the telling little expressions around his mouth, the powerful intelligence behind the vivid blue eyes that could be as sharp as razor blades, bright with sparkling amusement, dark with passion, soft with tender feeling.

They twinkled now with knowledge he was about to surprise her. "No. My first ambition was to be just like my grandfather. I was brought up on his ranch in Arizona. After my mother died, it was thought that I'd be better off with Grandfather Logan than in the care of nannies and housekeepers. You would have liked him, Rebecca. He was a cattle man through and through. No amount of oil riches was ever going to seduce him into a different way of life. When oil was drilled on his land, Grandfather Logan just moved from Texas to Arizona, set up another ranch and let my father deal with the oil business and everything else."

Slade shook his head in fond remembrance. "I really loved that old man. That's why I renamed Devil's Elbow for him. We bought that property just a few months after he died."

Rebecca hid a painful stab of disappointment Slade had not retained the ambition to be a cattleman like his grandfather. If he had... But that kind of wishful thinking had no place in their relationship. She now understood his concern over the cattle when she had confronted him in New York. It was a hangover from his youth. She told herself very firmly that the present and the future were in a totally different arena for Slade Cordell. She had no right to want or hope for anything from Slade after this week, yet...

"How old were you when you left your grandfather's ranch?" she asked, wondering if he had ever regretted not following in his grandfather's footsteps.

"Sixteen. My father thought it was time to start grooming me to take my place in the organisation he had built up."

"Did you want to go?"

"Yes," he answered without hesitation. "It seemed like an exciting new challenge. I wanted to see all that the big wide world had to offer. I guess I was ready to move on."

As he would move on from her, Rebecca sternly reminded herself. "You never went back?" she asked to put the matter beyond all possible doubt.

"Only to see Grandfather Logan. I don't go back now, although he left the ranch to me. It doesn't feel the same without him in his rocking chair on the porch. It's...empty, I guess."

Like Wildjanna had been without Gran, Rebecca thought. But it wouldn't stay empty. Not with another generation.

"I guess you're happy doing what you're doing, running Cordell Enterprises," she said matter-of-factly, forcing herself to face that reality once again.

Slade didn't immediately agree with her. It seemed to Rebecca that Slade's face settled into a look of brooding discontent. Then she remembered the problems arising from

Dan Petrie's enforced removal from the organisation. Slade had a lot of reorganising waiting on his plate. Then suddenly he relaxed and grinned at her.

"What I really wanted to be was an astrophysicist," he declared, his eyes twinkling at her startled bemusement.

"What's that?" she had to ask.

"Oh, someone who studies the stars, astronomy, the whole mystery of the universe. An astrophysicist tries to work out where we came from, where we are, what we are at and how the world and the universe will develop in the future." He gave a deprecating laugh. "If we're not all blown to bits by power-hungry politicians or some megalomaniac."

"That worries you?" It seemed a strange mixture of idealism and cynicism, hope and despair, and she wanted to know more about the way Slade thought.

"Where we are in five or ten billion years' time is fairly academic. But it does interest me and it does matter to me. Except for my father, and what he did, that's what I would have done with my life. I would have enjoyed tussling with the conceptual problems that are involved."

"And you can't do it now?"

He gave her a rueful little smile. "I'm probably more effective at making money. Cordell Enterprises funds a satellite doing basic research. That's as important as the work. Essential for getting the work done. Funds for such research are not easy to come by. Someone's got to provide them."

"But you're getting no personal satisfaction out of it."

He shook his head. "That doesn't really matter. It's that kind of work that's important. Human beings worry me. Why are we the way we are? Why do we fight? The wars, man's inhumanity to man..." He threw her a sharp look of irony. "Which, over the ages, has only been exceeded by man's inhumanity to women. I can't undo what's been done. But yes, it worries me, where we're all heading..."

He was a big man in far more ways than Rebecca had recognised. And a good man, as well. She could no longer believe he was a callous womaniser, or that he exploited anyone at all. A man who could be interested in the fate of the human race in five to ten billion years' time... She suddenly felt very privileged to know Slade Cordell, to have him share so much with her. She might not have much time with him but it was time well spent.

She leaned over and kissed him with a warm fervour that came straight from her heart. "That's for being what you are. The inner you," she said, smiling into his eyes. "And now I'm going to make love to you."

"Rebecca..." He said her name with a deep yearning that tugged at her soul, and the look in his eyes made her ache in anticipation of the loss that was inevitably coming.

She placed a finger on his lips, silencing the words that could not lead anywhere. All they had was now, and she began caressing him in the ways she had learnt gave him the most exquisite pleasure. When he could bear it no longer, she straddled him to take him inside her and felt both humbled and exalted by the look in his eyes as he watched her bring them both to an ecstatic fulfilment, which seemed more poignant than ever before.

THE LAST DAY FINALLY CAME, bringing with it a sharper appreciation of every moment left to them. Neither Rebecca nor Slade made mention of it. They didn't have to. A tension grew between them as the day wore to a close. Slade suggested a walk along the beach—their last walk together, although it wasn't acknowledged as such, not in words.

They walked a long way. Dying waves trickled around their feet. The footprints they made receded into the wet

sand, wiped away by a natural force as surely and relentlessly as other forces were about to tear them apart. The sun
that had shone so benevolently on them all week was a low-
ering yellow ball in a sky that was already gathering the
shades of the brief tropical twilight.

It was Slade who stopped walking first. Rebecca halted a
pace ahead of him, turned reluctantly, sensing the burden
on his mind and knowing there was no answer to it. His eyes
were dark with a turbulence that twisted her heart.

"I can't ignore my responsibilities, Rebecca," he said
quietly.

"I know. I want to thank you for—"

"Don't!" The harsh command instantly cut off the
speech that had been hovering on her lips. "You have
nothing to thank me for. You've given me . . ."

He paused to take a deep breath. "Is it any use asking you
to come with me?"

It hurt to say it but there was no evading the truth. "I
have things to do, too, Slade," she said softly. "My life is
here."

He nodded, looked out to sea for several nerve-wrenching
moments, then slowly turned his gaze to her. "There is no
hope then, is there, Rebecca?"

It was a plea scraped from a need that she couldn't hon-
estly fulfil. And if she tried, it would be a betrayal of herself. He knew that. It was written in his eyes even as he asked
the question of her. It was more a statement, edged with
despairing resignation, than a question.

"We each have our paths to take," she replied flatly. "I
couldn't be happy in New York, Slade. It would suffocate
me."

His mouth thinned as if forcibly holding back any further argument. His eyes seared her with barely restrained

wanting. "I'll miss you." Short, punched-out words that thudded into her heart.

"I'll miss you," she whispered. And to herself she added, more than I can ever tell you.

"Tell me what you intend to do over the next few months," he said gruffly. "I want to know. When I think about you... I want to know."

"There's a project that Gran and I used to discuss a lot. I want to set it up and get it operational. It's an ideal, I suppose, but now that Gran has gone... It's like a legacy that she wanted to pass on. And I intend to do that."

She swallowed to clear the choking well of grief in her throat, then tried to explain the feelings that she had shared with her grandmother. "Most of the Australian population live around the coastline, and the outback is like a dream centre of tradition that few ever really experience. Yet I doubt there's one Australian who can deny at least a subconscious fascination with it, a wanting to be part of it for however short a time."

"Like our old American West," Slade murmured appreciatively.

"Perhaps. You know your country better than I do. Gran wanted—I want—to set up a program where children whose lives have been limited, who, for one reason or other, only have a short time left to live, can come to Wildjanna and have that dream answered. This is something we can give, and Gran thought—I think—it might help those children. On Wildjanna, the cycle of life, the cycle of nature is so apparent. There's a timelessness that you become part of. The Aborigines understood it so clearly; the dream time; the melding of life and land; primitive, perhaps, but elemental..."

"Yes, elemental," Slade repeated, looking at her with eyes that seemed to attach that word and all its shades of meaning to her.

Rebecca's chest was suddenly so tight that it was a struggle to breath. She tore her gaze from his and looked out to sea—the vast shifting tide of water that supported and generated its own cycle of life, complementing the land.

"I have to make contact with medical—hospital—authorities," she said, forcing herself to ignore the pain inside her. "I know it will take time to make the availability of a stay on Wildjanna known to families who can benefit from it. And I have other preparations to make. The dam that Gran and I planned, just below the homestead. I've got to get it done before the drought breaks. It will become a large lake and attract all the wonderful birdlife of the outback, cockatoos, brolgas..."

She heaved a sigh and turned her gaze to Slade. "You've just seen the country at its worst. But after it rains, Slade, it's like a magical regeneration. The birds and wildflowers and animals that suddenly appear... It's as if God has waved His hand and performed another act of creation. To see it happen... If I could show that to children who have never seen life beyond the cities and will die in those godforsaken places without ever..."

She bit down on her tongue. Slade's life was city-bound. She didn't want to be offensively critical, particularly when he was achieving things she could never achieve.

"I'm sorry," she whispered. "I didn't mean..."

"I know what you meant, Rebecca," he assured her, his eyes dark with a deep appreciation of what she was saying.

Encouraged, she went on. "Anyway, I want to get started on setting up the project. I'll need to arrange some kind of funding to alleviate travelling costs for the children and their families. After the drought breaks, when times are better, I'll be able to manage something myself, but..."

"Cordell Enterprises will supply the funds, Rebecca."

She stared at him, taking in the resolute purpose in his eyes, yet inwardly recoiling from it.

"Slade, I wasn't asking, wasn't hinting..."

"I know you weren't, but I want to do it. Won't you share this with me? If only for the children's sake?"

Put that way, it was impossible to refuse his offer. And at heart she didn't want to. In a deeply personal way, the project would be like a memorial of what they had shared together.

"Thank you," she said simply. "It will be money well spent, Slade. I'm sure of it."

He smiled. "So am I." The smile faded into a look of concerned consideration. "It's not easy to cope with suffering children, Rebecca. They need such special care. You will need medical equipment, trained nurses, perhaps even doctors on hand."

"I'll solve those problems when I come to them," she said determinedly. "Gran and I worked on how best to meet the situation. I'll cope."

He frowned. "What about yourself? It won't be easy on your emotions."

"I know." She sighed. She looked at the sun, sinking so quickly now, as it was sinking too quickly on so many people who didn't know how to cope with life because they had never had any understanding of the nature of it. "But when has anything worthwhile ever been easy, Slade?"

She turned to him with a resolute little smile.

His mouth slowly curved in response. "You have no fear, have you?"

She shook her head. "I have fears, just like everyone else."

"They don't show."

"I really hate flying," she admitted.

"But you do it," Slade said softly.

"I do what has to be done. We both do, Slade. We share that in common."

He stared at her for what seemed like aeons of time. Then he stepped forward and wrapped her in his arms, crushing her against him in a silent agony of need that dismissed everything else. His mouth swept over her hair again and again, trailing feverish little kisses through the thick silky tresses.

"Let's go back," he rasped. "We still have the night."

Although they barely slept at all, the dawn rushed in on them long before they were ready to face it. Packing their things and seeing that the cottage was left in reasonable order were mechanical tasks that added a sharper edge of sadness to their imminent parting. A car arrived to take them to the airport. They sat in the back seat, Slade's fingers laced tightly through hers, and neither spoke a word all the way. There was nothing left to say.

When they reached the airport, Slade turned to Rebecca, his face strained, his eyes roving hungrily over her face.

"Stay in the car, Rebecca. I'll instruct the driver to take you into Brisbane. Just tell him where you want to go."

"All right," she agreed, aware that the waiting for his flight to be called would be unbearable to both of them.

He curled one hand around her cheek, tilting her face to his, and he kissed her with such loving tenderness that she could barely hold back the tears.

"I'll come back when I can, Rebecca," he murmured, his voice rough with suppressed feeling. His eyes burnt fiercely into hers. His fingers stroked one last caress on her cheek. Then he opened the car door and left her.

She didn't watch him pick up his bag and stride away. She stared straight ahead, seeing nothing, forcing her mind to recite the steps she now had to take. She did not yet know if she was pregnant with Slade's child. Her child. Their child. She could only hope she was.

And for the first time she did not think of that child as the fourth generation for Wildjanna. More than anything else at that moment, the baby—if one had been conceived—was part of Slade Cordell, and she fiercely wanted it to be so.

CHAPTER TEN

SLADE CORDELL only half-listened to Bert Hinkman expounding on what effect the latest tanker accident would have on oil prices. He was remembering the environmental tragedy resulting from the '89 accident when the *Exxon Valdez* ran aground, spilling two hundred and forty thousand barrels of oil into the sea off the coast of Alaska, blackening beaches, coating plant and marine life, killing....

A savage wave of revulsion swept through him. *What in hell are we doing to this planet,* he thought, *all in the holy name of keeping every machine running.* Human error, mechanical error, computer error... releasing forces of destruction that pollute the land and the sea and the air.

He rose restlessly from his chair behind the black marble desk and walked over to the wall of plate glass to stare broodingly at the man-made monoliths of Manhattan. Rebecca was right. This concrete jungle had no soul. Ambition, but no soul. The world was becoming more and more a godforsaken place, and where would it all end?

Rebecca...

The need for her ripped through him like a knife. He barely stifled a groan. As it was, Hinkman was probably wondering what he had said wrong to have provoked this impolite interruption to his dissertation. Slade recollected himself and turned to face him again.

Bert Hinkman was one of the best of the board members, not only efficient but completely dependable. He had been on the board in Blair Cordell's time and did his job with meticulous care. He liked it, took pride in his performance, and unfortunately for Slade, had no ambition to move any higher. More than ever now, that high-backed leather chair in the boardroom felt like a millstone around Slade's neck.

His mouth moved stiffly into an apologetic smile. "Sorry, Bert. My mind wandered. Please go on."

"If you'll pardon my saying so, Slade, it's time you eased up a bit," the older man advised. "For the past four months, ever since you came back from Australia, you've been hard at it, revamping the organisation and setting up a new network of accountability. I won't say it didn't need doing, but you've been driving yourself to get it done."

He paused, then added in pointed concern, "When was the last time you had a full night's sleep?"

Slade gave a dismissive shrug and walked to his desk. He consciously tried to relax as he sat down again. Unless he knocked himself out with sleeping pills, a habit he did not want to fall into, he hated going to bed. It reminded him too painfully of what he didn't have—couldn't have.

"Quite frankly, you look like hell. Drawn and tired and— if I might be so bold—you're also uncharacteristically short of temper," Hinkman said with a telling little grimace.

"Getting a bad reputation, am I?" Slade asked wearily.

"No. I wouldn't say that," came the considering reply. "You're well-liked on the whole. And sometimes a short temper can move things along better than all the pleasant reasoning in the world. I merely mention it because it's given rise to some concern amongst those who know you. It's just not like you, Slade."

"I'll try to ease off, Bert." The trouble was, impatience was eating into him. He wanted everything running smoothly as fast as possible. He wanted to go back to Rebecca. He wanted...

"Do you want to hear the rest of my report, or shall I—"

"Yes, yes," Slade cut in, consciously softening the second yes as he heard the sharp edge on the first. "Please continue," he added gently.

But he couldn't concentrate on what his executive was saying. Not for long. He heard snatches of the report, enough to make intelligible replies to questions, but his thoughts kept drifting to an entirely different world—the one that held Rebecca.

He desperately wanted to be with her again, but was it the right thing to do? The question often tortured him in the middle of the night. She wanted a child. If he went back could he deny her a child if she asked it of him? He had said that they would discuss it, but what kind of father could he be?

He'd be torn between both worlds, giving satisfaction in neither place. It wasn't fair to anyone, least of all to Rebecca—dropping in and out of her life whenever he could make the time. If he stayed away, maybe she would find someone who could give her the marriage she wanted, the kind of marriage she believed in.

But to stay away... Paul Neilsen had had the guts to set her free to tread her own path. But damn it all! Paul Neilsen couldn't give her what he could. Another month at most and he would have everything running in a responsible pattern. He could leave then. Take maybe as much as two months off to stay with her. If she let him set up a computer system at Wildjanna so that he could keep tabs on the figures coming in... maybe longer.

Was she feeling the same need for him or was she stronger than he was? Slade suspected she might be. Implacable, he had called her, and he could well imagine her shutting all thought of him out of her mind. He had been so tempted to call her, to keep her thinking of him, remembering; but he recognised it as a selfish urge. Self-indulgent. Greedy.

She had given him what he had asked of her, and she had chosen not to come with him. He should have realised there could be no other choice for her right from the beginning. Implacable, like the land that claimed her.

Apart from which, she still loved Paul Neilsen, and that damned wheelchair would always keep her tied to him. Slade fiercely wished Neilsen had crashed doing something other than saving Rebecca's life. Because of that she would always love Neilsen—yet she had locked that love away in a separate compartment while she had given herself to Slade. Was he now locked away in another compartment while she got on with her life?

Slade was almost sure that she had come to love him that week, maybe not the same kind of love she bore Paul Neilsen, but it had been something special to her. He couldn't doubt that. Was it enough for her to want again, to always want, even though it only came from time to time?

Could she accept a marriage like that?

Was he prepared to commit himself to a marriage like that?

To have her, to know he could always have her...yet it was so impossibly impractical! Slade bitterly castigated himself for having started something that he couldn't finish right. But not to have known her as he had, even feeling the anguished need for her that he did now, Slade knew in his heart that he would do the same thing again, anything at all, just to have had that one experience she had given him. And he couldn't bear not to go back to her, no matter what. In three or four weeks...

Slade shook his head to clear it of the endless treadmill of tormenting questions. He applied himself to listening to the end of Hinkman's report. As usual, it was succinct and penetrating. Slade gave the nod of approval to the recommendations offered and saw the older man out of his office.

Ease off, he recalled ruefully as he shut the door and turned towards the desk. It was well-meant advice but it was easier to bear the inner loneliness if he buried himself in work. Besides, there was so much that needed to be done.

Bert Hinkman had his responsibilities covered, but the rest... No, there was one other. Ross Harper, the new man on the board. He had promise. He definitely had promise. Sharp, efficient, one step ahead of the game. It had been the right decision bringing him in. New blood. Cordell Enterprises certainly needed an injection of that. If only Harper had more experience under his belt.

Slade heaved an impatient sigh. He couldn't expect too much too soon from a guy who was only just feeling his way, yet maybe Harper was a possibility for the future.

His mind drifted to Rebecca again, and her plans for the future. She had not yet applied to Cordell Enterprises for the funds needed for her project, but that didn't mean she wasn't busy with it. Such things took time to set up. He tried to picture where she would construct the dam that would become a lake. The drought had not broken, so she had certainly had the time to make the dam as big as she wanted it. He wished he had asked her more about it.

The telephone on his desk buzzed a summons, snapping him out of his musing. Get on with your own work, he told himself sternly, and strode over to snatch up the receiver. He hoped it wouldn't spew forth another problem that had to be resolved before he could leave.

"Mr. Cordell, there's a gentleman from Australia asking to see you. A Mr. Emilio Dalvarez. He says he only has today in New York—"

"Is he there with you?" Slade broke in, feeling as though a sledgehammer had hit his heart. Was something wrong at Wildjanna? Had something happened to Rebecca?

"Yes, sir."

"Bring him in immediately. I'll see him straightaway."

Slade paced the floor like a caged mountain lion as he waited for the Argentinian to be ushered in. Maybe the drought had caused more problems. Although if that was the case, Emilio could surely have communicated with him through the management at Devil's Elbow. During the week that Slade had spent there, he had neutralised all hostilities. He had left the man on friendly terms. There shouldn't be any problems that concerned Emilio Dalvarez enough to make a trip to New York.

A brief knock heralded the opening of his office door. Slade spun on his heel and moved swiftly to greet his unexpected visitor and offer an outstretched hand of welcome. "Emilio... it's good to see you," he said, hiding his inner tension as best he could, although instantly aware that the Argentinian was distinctly ill at ease.

A hard brown hand returned a tighter clasp than mere politeness required, but there was no assertion of superiority in it. Slade was sure it was more an expression of uncertainty, which disturbed him even further. Emilio Dalvarez was very much a man who would rarely be uncertain of anything.

"Mr. Cordell—Slade... I hope I am not imposing."

"Not at all. Please, come and sit down. We'll have a drink together. You can tell me all the news of what's been happening."

"No. No drink, thank you. I cannot stay long. I am flying on to Argentina this afternoon," Emilio stated. "The times have changed in my country. I'm allowed to go back for a short period. I am no longer an émigré. My father called for me to come. My mother is not well. I must go, you understand."

"Of course. I'm sorry that you've got problems," Slade sympathised. "I hope they are not too serious."

"Who is to know?" Emilio said philosophically. "My mother has lived a goodly span of years. Family is family. It is a long time since I have seen her. It is right that I go and be the son I am to her."

"Yes," Slade quickly agreed, then gestured an invitation to the grouping of sofas where Rebecca had sat with him so many months ago.

Emilio moved to one and sat with an air of great dignity. He wore a suit with considerable distinction, Slade thought, although his weathered face clearly denoted him as a man who worked outdoors. In his somewhat narrow way, Emilio Dalvarez commanded respect. He lived by his own lights, and Slade was not about to denigrate them. At the very least, Emilio had a sense of honour that was too rare a quality to be undervalued.

"This is a very impressive building," Emilio said, eyeing the plate-glass wall and its view over Manhattan. "I can now see that you have much to take into consideration."

It was a concession, but a concession to what? Slade decided it was up to him to take the bull by the horns. "Emilio..." He leaned forward from the seat he had taken opposite his visitor. "I realise your time is particularly valuable on this journey. As much as I am honoured by your visit, I feel sure you would not have broken your journey for idle chitchat with me. How is Rebecca?''

"As you left her!" came the sharp reply, edged with a hostile reproof that put Slade instantly on guard.

"What does that mean?" he asked, keeping his own voice steady and quiet.

"She is having your baby," came the unequivocal reply, stabbed home with a dark glare that expressed an angry frustration with the situation.

Slade was dumbstruck, dazed, his mind jagging between disbelief and the stark honest bluntness of Emilio's statement. His baby? The wonder of it. How had it happened? Why hadn't Rebecca rung him and told him?

"Rebecca Wilder is a proud independent woman. A strong woman," the Argentinian continued. "I hold her in high esteem, as I did her grandmother. She would never tell you, or ask anything of you. She will stand alone, that one." He glowered at Slade. "But to my mind, you have acted wrongly towards her. Badly wrong. To take such a woman, and not honour her enough to marry her. To leave her carrying your child—"

"Emilio, are you sure about this?" Slade broke in urgently. "I made her promise me she was protected..." But not all contraceptives were a hundred percent fail proof! And perhaps she had misled him. Or let him mislead himself.

Emilio snorted and stood up, drawing himself to his full height and looking down at Slade with contempt. "Are you denying that you are the father?"

"No!" Slade shot to his feet. "If Rebecca is carrying a child, it's mine. It has to be mine." He shook his head, still incredulous that it had actually happened. "I don't know how or why... you're certain that she is?"

"You are a man of the city," Emilio jeered. "There is no doubt in Rebecca's mind. What kind of soul do you have, to leave her like that?"

Had she deliberately lied to him? Slade's mind started reeling with implications. Had she told him what she knew he wanted to hear and cold-bloodedly gone ahead to use him for her own purpose? Was she that ruthless in forging her own destiny? Did she intend to go back to Paul Neilsen and... Slade's recoil from that thought was instant and violent. Not with *his* child! No other man was going to be the surrogate father of *his* child!

Emilio had stalked over to the glass wall, taken in the panoramic view with a sweep of his eyes, then turned his back on it, his face sternly judgemental as he glared at Slade. "I would have married her," he declared. "I offered to do so. But Rebecca Wilder is an honourable woman. She told me why she could not accept my offer. She told me why she would not accept any offer. I respect her for her honesty. But you... You think you can take the best of both worlds without any redress? I—" he thumped his chest with vehement feeling "—I think you are despicable, and I wanted to tell it to you straight to your face."

It was clear that his own personal disappointment in regard to Rebecca had lent fire to his sense of injustice. Slade could no longer doubt that Emilio Dalvarez had not only told him the truth, but the Argentinian also felt passionately enough about it to break his journey home to his family.

Whatever motives or intentions Rebecca had, now was not the time for Slade to question them. This man was hurt, and Slade had contributed largely to that hurt, albeit unintentionally. How deeply Emilio's feelings for Rebecca went was impossible to tell, but it behove Slade to tread carefully and not add insult to injury.

"Emilio," he began softly, appeasingly. "This news has come as a great shock to me. It must have come as a shock to you, too, when you first heard it. I'm sorry about that. I didn't know that you had anything more than neighbourly intentions in regard to Rebecca. Although even if I had known, in all honesty I could not have backed away from the attraction she holds for me."

"I do not begrudge you that," Emilio fired at him. "She is a woman who could attract any man. She has the right to take whom she chooses. But for you to take advantage and then to leave her!"

"My relationship with Rebecca . . . that's a private thing, Emilio," Slade said more strongly, giving vent to some of the feelings he was trying to control. "But believe me, I did not come to it lightly, nor do I intend to let it go lightly. Even as you arrived, I was planning to return to her as quickly as I could. There is still some urgent business here. But now it's far more imperative that I go to her. And I shall be on my way to Wildjanna as soon as possible. Whatever has happened there, I'll do what's necessary to clean up the mess I left behind. You have my word on it."

"I hope so. I feel outraged."

"So do I," Slade assured him emphatically.

"You must have known what you were doing!"

"There are times when a man stops thinking, Emilio."

The anger simmered down to a grudging understanding, but there was still a lot of dark reservation in his eyes. "I hope your brains are now back in place," he said sternly.

"They will be by the time I get there. I appreciate what you've done, Emilio. I thank you, sincerely, for taking the time and the trouble to come to me. It is the act of a good neighbour, and I'll always be mindful of the service you've done me."

Emilio ruminated over those sentiments for several moments before giving an approving nod. "As a neighbour to both of you, it was my duty to speak to you."

"I couldn't agree more. I'm very grateful to you," Slade said with enough fervour to satisfy any of Emilio's lingering grievances.

In truth, Slade *was* deeply grateful to him, but he was anxious to get moving and he needed to get Emilio moving first. The sense of loss—that Rebecca had chosen not to share this with him—was intense and mind-shattering. He had to go to her. That it was his duty wasn't the issue at all. He wanted to go anyway. He needed to think. He realised he was still shocked, deeply shocked by Emilio's reservations. Somehow he had to find a way...

Filled with a tearing sense of urgency he thrust out his hand, and was greatly relieved when Emilio took it with barely a hesitation. Slade ushered him to the door with a few more polite platitudes and they parted on terms of mutual respect.

His first call was to book a seat on the first flight to Brisbane. Then he called in his secretary and dictated at top speed. The man would have to come with him. He needed someone who was familiar with his work practices. He put out a few critical memos for each of his divisional managers as a holding action, particularising those areas that had not yet received his personal attention and demanding appropriate adjustments.

Until he could get back to New York he would have to trust others to fulfil the various criteria of responsibility outlined. His own personal feeling—barely suppressed—was that Cordell Enterprises could go to hell and he wouldn't give a damn, but an edge of sanity insisted that he couldn't desert the ship without any authority at all. As it was, he would be leaving it at a critical time for an indefinite period, but he had to go!

It was his child!

He had to know what was on Rebecca's mind. Why had she done it?

The pregnancy was a reality. Four months! A child on the way—halfway to being born. While Slade had never given having children a great deal of priority in his life before, somehow it was totally different now.

His son.

Or daughter.

His flesh and blood, and Rebecca's...

The rest of the world could go hang!

He was going to Wildjanna, and he was going to stay there and make sure everything turned out right. This was real life he was dealing with, not figures on papers or hypothetical reasoning. It was the life of his child! And he sure as heck was going to have some say in it! A great deal of say in it, if he got anything like his way at all.

Knowing Rebecca as he did, his say mightn't amount to very much. But one thing was certain. She was going to know that he was there to be counted!

CHAPTER ELEVEN

REBECCA LOWERED THE SCOOP of the bulldozer, changed gears and slowly reversed down the bank of the dam, the back edge of the scoop dragging over the loose dirt, smoothing the slope to a more eye-pleasing line. Then she trundled the bulldozer up to repeat the process.

The important part of the work had been done weeks ago. The structure of the lake had been carved out of the land. It could rain any time it liked and the massive banks would hold the water. What she was doing was purely cosmetic, but she wanted the end result to look as perfectly natural as possible.

The station hands had done the really heavy earth shifting and building. Rebecca had eased off her own workload once she was certain of her pregnancy, but for this hour each evening, after the heat of the day was passed, she liked to work on the finishing touches herself. Apart from the aesthetic purpose, it also served to tire her out physically before she retired for the night.

Memories tended to crowd in on her once she went to bed. Sometimes it was hard to get to sleep. She missed Slade—desperately missed all they had shared together—yet she didn't regret what she had done. Already the baby growing inside her had dispelled so much of the lonely emptiness that had threatened her personal existence. She looked forward to its birth with a wonderfully uplifting sense of joy.

Even Milly was not so cross-faced about it any more. Emilio, however, was another kettle of fish. Rebecca hoped that his trip to Argentina would take the edge off his disappointment. She hoped that while he was there he might even find another wife.

She reached the bottom of the slope again and changed gears to start the next run. She glanced up to position her line of approach to a neat parallel with the last grade and caught sight of a man jogging around the top of the bank, waving both arms above his head in an obvious signal to grab her attention. She put the machine on idle, waiting to find out what he wanted. She couldn't figure out who it was. He was too big to be . . .

Shock pummelled Rebecca's heart. Only one man she knew was that big; the towering height, the broad shoulders, the lithe muscular body, the long powerful legs eating up the distance between them. She whipped off her hat and then the goggles that protected her eyes from the dust the dozer kicked up. He was on top of the rise just above her now and there was no mistaking who it was. Slade Cordell had come back!

Rebecca sat there completely dazed by the sight of him plunging down the slope towards her. She hadn't really believed Slade would ever return. It had seemed far more logical that once back in his own world, he would recognise that their week together was the fantasy it had been—time out of time for both of them. Anything else between them was simply not practical. Yet he was here! It was him!

Before Rebecca could recollect herself enough to greet him, or even move, he had swung himself onto the dozer, switched off the ignition key and was hauling her out of the seat, setting her feet on the ground, the vivid blue eyes dark with a turbulence of feeling that swirled around her, constricting her throat, her chest, so that all she could do was stare dumbly at him.

"What on earth are you thinking of, Rebecca?" he cried harshly, his hands squeezing her upper arms, fingers digging bruises in some terrible agitation of spirit. "Don't be such a fool! For God's sake! Consider the baby!"

The baby? He knew about the baby? But how could he?

He groaned and released her arms. He swept one hand around her waist to pull her none too gently against him. The other he lifted to her face, tremulously brushing away the untidy wisps of hair that had come loose from the tie at the back of her neck. I'm a dirty mess, she thought dimly, but Slade wasn't looking at her as though she were a dirty mess. His eyes hungered into hers with soul-stirring force.

"Say you're glad to see me," he rasped. "Say you missed me as much as I missed you. Say something. Anything, Rebecca."

It felt so good to be pressed to the length and strength of his body again. It felt wonderful to have him holding her, touching her. "Kiss me," she whispered.

His chest heaved against her tender breasts and then his mouth was on hers, feasting on hers, starving for the sweet devastating passion that flared so quickly between them. Rebecca responded with a fierce hunger of her own, wanting to drown in all the wildly pulsing sensations he aroused in her, wanting to obliterate all the hows and whys and wherefores, and exult only in the fact that he was with her again, giving her more of himself.

All these months she had forced up walls of logic to protect herself from yearning for such a moment as this, and now she didn't care that they came crashing down. She could build them again later. When she had to. But no way was she going to stint on this incredible reality. She revelled in Slade's kisses and clung to him in sheer boneless wanting. If it was madness, then it was a madness she willingly embraced.

He tucked her head onto his shoulder, keeping it gently pressed there as he fought the violent tremor that shook his body. His breathing was harsh and irregular, his arms still crushing her to him. His cheek rubbed over her hair in a soft mindless yearning as shaky bursts of words spilled from his heart.

"I've wanted you so much. I haven't stopped wanting you. Not for one day, one hour, one second ... an agony of wanting. All this time, endless days and nights, waiting to get back to you...."

Rebecca could not disbelieve him. His voice throbbed with the truth of what he was saying. His body throbbed its own confirmation even more convincingly. Her mind throbbed with the wonder of it.

"Slade," she whispered, for the sheer pleasure of saying his name.

"Why didn't you call me, Rebecca? Why didn't you let me know about the baby? I would have come sooner."

She sighed, realising once again that life didn't really work by logic at all. "You didn't want a baby, Slade," she reminded him softly.

He tilted her head back to search her eyes, his own reflecting an intense inner turmoil. "You must know I would care, Rebecca."

It was plain that he did care. Very deeply. Yet that first day in his New York office, he had given her the impression that having children was not important to him, that he could live quite happily without ever concerning himself over what a child of his own might mean to him. He had even offered to father one for her so that there would be no impediment to her marrying Paul. Although he had seemed to change his mind about that after she had given in to him.

"You did think that I wouldn't care," he said in a voice that sounded strangely hollow.

"Slade . . ." She reached up and stroked the taut muscles in his cheek. "It was my decision. And it wouldn't have been right for me to impose anything you didn't want on your life. Not something you'd never planned on doing."

"I said we'd discuss it, Rebecca," he reminded her, still deeply disturbed.

"You said a lot of things, Slade," she said softly. "And then quickly backtracked on them after I conceded what you wanted."

"No. You misunderstood."

She shook her head. "Maybe it changed for you in the week we had together. It did for me. But you held out something to me that day—over my grandmother's grave— and then you took it away, promising only a possibility in the future. I made my choice then, Slade, because I didn't trust you to come back and deliver what you'd promised me. And I gave you what you wanted in return."

The flesh beneath her fingertips contracted. "Was that all it was for you, Rebecca? A return for services rendered?"

"No. You know it wasn't." She smiled. "What am I doing here in your arms, kissing you like there's no tomorrow?"

"There is a tomorrow. We'll make a tomorrow," he said vehemently.

"Because of the baby?" Her smile slipped into sad irony. "How did you know about it, Slade? Did Milly blurt it out when you called at the homestead?"

"No. Emilio told me. He stopped off in New York on his way to Argentina."

That piece of news slapped into her face like a wet fish. Emilio confronting Slade in his office, puffed up with moral righteousness. Rebecca's insides deflated into a sick queasiness. Her arms limply withdrew from around Slade's neck. Her gaze dropped to stare miserably, sightlessly, over Slade's shoulder.

"I'm sorry. He had no right. No right at all," she said in bitter condemnation, knowing precisely how Emilio would have carried on, demanding that Slade make some reparation to the woman he had dishonoured.

Tears welled in her eyes. It must be the pregnancy making her weak, she thought. She hadn't expected Slade to come back. He had only come now in some stupid burst of guilt over the baby. If only Emilio Dalvarez had minded his own damned business ...

She gave an anguished jerk of her head as Slade grasped her chin to turn it to him. "I'm all right!" she insisted blindly. "I'm fine! I don't need you, Slade Cordell! You didn't have to come. You're making this worse for me than it has to be."

She tore herself out of his embrace and lurched towards the bulldozer. A hand caught at her arm and she beat it away. "Don't touch me!" she hurled at him as she backed up against the machine and forced some stiffening down her spine.

Her shoulders squared to a dignified bearing. A bitter pride sparked through the moisture in her eyes. Her chin lifted in defiant rejection of her earlier susceptibility to Slade's physical magnetism. That her face and clothes were streaked with dirt made no whit of difference. She knew who she was. She knew where she was going. Her own rigid sense of destiny was stamped on every taut line of her face and body.

"Rebecca ..." Slade stepped towards her, his hands raised in urgent appeal.

"No! Keep your distance, Slade," she demanded, steel spearing through the shakiness of her voice. "I won't have you using my—our—mutual attraction to mess up something that is completely clear-cut. I never counted on you turning up in my life again. If Emilio hadn't interfered—''

''I was coming anyway,'' he broke in vehemently. ''Ever since I left you I've been working towards coming back to you. The only difference Emilio made was that I'm here sooner than I would have made it otherwise.''

''How much sooner?'' Rebecca pounced.

''A month, give or take a week,'' he returned impatiently.

''In that case, you just go back to your work, Slade. The baby and I are doing fine. We don't need you here. We don't need you to come back, either. A month will give you time to realise that you have no responsibility to this child whatsoever. I took full responsibility for it before it was even conceived.''

''I'm supposed to ignore it, am I, Rebecca?'' he asked in that soft-dangerous voice of his. ''I'm supposed to leave you to your own devices and forget all about both you and the child? Is that it?''

The glittering determination in his eyes told her that his questions were purely rhetorical. It wouldn't matter what she replied, he was not going to be swayed from the course he had decided upon. She stared at him, recognising the same mesmerising force she had felt that day in the graveyard when Slade had issued his challenge, and it seemed that her world was collapsing in on her. He emitted waves of power that both threatened and tugged at her soul.

''Well, I can tell you this,'' he continued quietly. ''Hell will freeze over first. You made the decision, but it's my child as much as yours. And I'm staying, Rebecca. We have offices in Brisbane and I've left my secretary there to set up a communications headquarters. As and when I'm needed to deal with business, I'll commute to Brisbane from Wildjanna. Or from Devil's Elbow if you're too stiff-necked to admit you want me with you every bit as much as I want to be with you.''

He paused, inviting a response from her, but Rebecca was too amazed by his resolute organisation of his affairs to think clearly at all.

Slade pressed on, driving his points home. ''Either way, Rebecca, I'm not going back to New York until we get our relationship sorted out. Somehow or other, there's going to be some giving and taking. The thing that's going to be sorted out is who are the takers and who are the givers.''

Ruthless and relentless, Rebecca thought, yet strangely enough his declaration eased the sickening turmoil stirred by the knowledge of Emilio's unwarranted betrayal of her confidence. She felt a welling of pleasurable excitement that Slade so totally refused to be turned away. Nevertheless, the measures he had taken, and would take for the purpose of staying with her, could only be temporary. Apart from which, this time they could not put their separate lives on hold, as they had at Forty-Mile Beach.

''It won't work, Slade,'' she said bluntly. ''You're a taker, and I'm not much good at giving. However, since you insist you want to stay, and you've gone to so much trouble about it, then stay. But have no expectations, Slade. It won't work for long. This isn't your life, and I won't accept you imposing standards and values on me that are not my own.''

''I think it's up to me to decide what I want my life to be, Rebecca,'' he retorted, totally unshaken in his determination. In fact, the look in his eyes had intensified to a blaze of possessiveness. ''There are two things I am sure of,'' he stated. ''I want you in it. And I want our child in it. I haven't yet had time to work out the rest, but first and foremost, I want you to marry me. That comes first, Rebecca. Then somehow we'll forge a new life.''

"Because of the baby?" She shook her head incredulously, her eyes filling with scorn. "That's Emilio talking, Slade. You should know better. You should know me better. There's no way I'll marry you."

She couldn't afford to. If Slade wanted his child in his life, if she married him he would have a legal claim. He could take the child away from her when their marriage broke up under the inevitable pressures of their separate ways of life.

No way would she ever give him the power to do that. He had offered, she had taken, and she would fight Slade to the death if he tried to change his deal with her.

He moved towards her, each step slow and deliberate, and Rebecca had the strong sensation that nothing she said or did would hold him back this time. "That week we had together was the best week I ever had in my life. It wasn't just me, Rebecca. We shared something that few people even get near." His hands lifted and curled lightly around her shoulders, his eyes burning into hers. "Can you deny that?"

"No. But it doesn't change the situation we have now," she said forcefully, desperate to block the effect his closeness had on her. She was not going to waver over this. To give in would be a madness that encompassed far more than any brief physical or emotional satisfaction.

"I know it's not an ideal situation, but there are plenty of other marriages that survive long separations because of work. It makes the times together all the more special," Slade argued seductively. "It can be so with us, Rebecca."

She refused to let the idea take hold. It was a temptation she couldn't possibly nurture in any way. It could only lead to terribly destructive futures for both of them. And their child.

"You said marriage would never work for you, Slade," she fiercely reminded him.

"I'll *make* this marriage work. Whatever it takes."

"What you feel about the baby...it will pass. It's a *novelty* to you. Just as I was a novelty to you. If you'd ever really wanted a child in your life, you'd have made a way to have one before this. You're not thinking straight, Slade."

"I said those things before I really knew you, or myself, Rebecca. Don't hold them against me. Not now. Please, consider what I'm saying right here at this time."

Every instinct rebelled against any persuasion. Her voice was harsh with a violent clash of emotion as she replied. "No. I won't, Slade. I won't ever consider a marriage with you. We don't have enough together to consider a marriage. Not a lifetime marriage. You can't even begin to give me what I had with Paul. Stay with me as long as you like, but don't talk marriage to me. Let there be no feeling of obligation between us. That will sour our relationship faster than anything else. When you want to go, go."

His face tightened. His fingers dug into her shoulders. Then as if he realised what he was doing he made a savage grimace and pulled his hands away. Rebecca's heart dropped like a stone when he stepped back, swung on his heel and left her without another word spoken. He trudged up the dam wall and stood on the bank, apparently looking out over the whole expanse of the excavation.

As much as she ached to, Rebecca did not call out to beg him to stay with her, but her eyes clung to his dark silhouette, willing him not to go. It seemed to her there was a defeated droop to his shoulders and she grieved over hurting him. He had come to her in good faith—mistaken good faith—and in time he would see that her rejection of his proposal was no more nor less than solid common sense. However, that was probably no balm to his wounded pride right now.

It had taken every reserve of strength she had to reject his impulsive proposal. She wanted him so much. Wanted him with her for the rest of her life. But the reality was she could never have him like that. And she dared not risk giving him any legal right to take their child away from her.

Rebecca had to wait until her legs felt strong enough to follow him. He didn't move. He didn't even glance at her when she finally stood beside him. His face could have been carved of stone. Rebecca released a shaky breath and tried to speak in a calm voice.

"Milly will be preparing dinner. You're welcome to stay, Slade," she stated quietly.

"Crumbs, Rebecca?" He sliced her a tortured look that stabbed straight at her heart.

"Roast beef, more likely," she snapped reflexively. If he couldn't see that she was saving them both from intolerable stresses in rejecting his proposal, then he was unbelievably blind. "Please yourself," she added dully.

"Oh, I'll come," he drawled, the pain in his eyes overlaid with a dangerous glitter as he turned to her. "I'll take everything you offer me, Rebecca. I need some return for being used . . . once again."

The blood drained from Rebecca's face as she realised he was likening her to all the women in his past. "You got what you asked for, Slade," she justified weakly.

"Answer me one thing!" he answered venomously. "Do you intend to use my child to get Paul Neilsen to marry you?"

Nausea rolled through her stomach. "No," she choked out, fighting dizzying waves in her head. "It was you who suggested that, Slade. Not me. Never me."

"But you still love him," Slade said bitterly. "That's why you won't marry me, isn't it?"

"No. It's not. I'm sorry if you can't understand. I'm sorry." She felt herself swaying. "I have to sit down."

She dropped to the ground and had her head between her knees before Slade had time to react to her startling action. Black dots were dancing before her eyes, her face felt clammy, and the earth was whirling around, but she managed to stay conscious.

"Rebecca!" The sharp concern in Slade's voice penetrated the fog in her mind, and she was vaguely aware of him hunkered down beside her.

"Bit faint. That's all," she explained jerkily.

He muttered something savage but she couldn't make it out. Then she found herself being lifted up and cradled against his chest.

"Better on the ground," she protested.

"Better in bed," he said grimly, and started striding towards the homestead.

She managed to slide a hand around his neck and he hoisted her a bit higher so that her head rested comfortably on his shoulder. It felt so good to have Slade holding her again that Rebecca didn't protest any further.

"I'm sorry, Rebecca," he said in a pained voice. "I'm a darned fool, upsetting you like that. I came to take care of you, not..." A self-contemptuous sound gravelled from his throat. "Brains still in the wrong place!"

"Yes," she agreed.

He gave a harsh little laugh. "No. Not there. Not right now anyway. And I don't care if they're crumbs. Crumbs are better than nothing. Besides, I'll show you we've got more in common than you realise. You just wait and see, Rebecca Wilder. I'll show you. You're not going to get rid of me as fast as you think."

"Don't want to get rid of you," she mumbled, feeling snugly warm as her circulation surged back into action. She would take all he would give her, too. Crumbs. Anything.

Until he left again. "I like you showing me things," she added as an afterthought.

"You're not to get into that bone-shaking bulldozer again," he said sternly. "You tell me what you want done and I'll do it."

"Can you drive a dozer?"

"I'll learn," he said grimly.

"Can you do any of the things I'll want done?"

"I'll learn," he said even more grimly.

Rebecca thought about that. She wasn't going to let Slade boss her around. On the other hand, as long as Slade stayed with her, she wouldn't have the problem of getting to sleep. She decided there was some compromising that would be acceptable.

"All right," she agreed. "I'll let you learn."

Slade breathed a satisfied little sigh.

Rebecca burrowed her face into the warmth of his throat and resolved not to think about the future. She didn't know and she didn't want to know how long Slade would stay with her this time. She would simply take each day as it came and make the most of it. At least they had got one thing settled. He didn't have to feel obliged to marry her any more. In fact, marriage was completely out of the question. She hoped Slade accepted that.

CHAPTER TWELVE

THEY HAD TWENTY-THREE incredibly marvellous days together. Rebecca knew exactly because she marked each day Slade was with her on the calendar in her office.

Not quite every hour was spent in each other's company. Slade needed an office also, and one of the spare rooms in the homestead was set up for this purpose. He had brought with him a teleprinter, a fax machine and a lot of other electronic communications equipment. Most days he was in touch with Brisbane, and occasionally he got up in the middle of the night to speak to his people in New York. These hours on his business became part of their routine and Rebecca did not interfere. Sometimes she fantasised that this arrangement was a permanent solution, but in her saner moments she recognised that as a pipe dream. It was only a Band-Aid solution, which could not possibly hold for long.

Milly, of course, looked down her long nose at the whole affair, until Slade told her categorically that it wasn't *his* fault they weren't married. Whereupon the wiry little housekeeper eyed him with much more favour and reserved her long-nosed look for Rebecca, who was not acting with the propriety that her grandmother would have expected of her. Rebecca happily ignored both Slade's claim and Milly's terse little reproofs. Each day was too precious to her to waste any second of it in argument.

Slade learnt to drive the bulldozer. Not very well, but well enough. She sat up on the bank and directed his labours, much to both their satisfactions. He wasn't too keen on her riding out to check the cattle on horseback, but he reluctantly conceded that there were places where a Land Rover couldn't be driven. He rode with her. He would learn how to check whatever she wanted checked. It was only a question of becoming more familiar with this land and its unique peculiarities. After all, he *had* been brought up on a ranch.

He suffered saddle soreness without complaint, declaring it was well worth it to have Rebecca rub liniment into him. In fact, he was perfectly content to invite soreness every night. It was getting to be mighty erotic. It gave him ideas he'd never had before, and sometimes Rebecca didn't finish massaging in the liniment before he had to show them to her. She didn't think it was worth protesting. Slade could make her forget anything when he set his mind on it. When they did eventually slide into sleep, they slept very well.

Whenever Rebecca stopped to think about what was happening, she only felt confused. Slade did not appear to be at all bored or discontented with the life they led. He really seemed to enjoy being part of Wildjanna. Yet she could not accept that it would stay that way for a lifetime. Whether it was simply another challenge for him, a complete break away from his other life, or perhaps a pleasurable recollection of his boyhood with his grandfather, she didn't know and she didn't want to ask.

However, she was all too poignantly aware that Slade was carving a deeper place in her heart with every hour he spent sharing her life. She was afraid to even think how she would feel when he left her to resume his real life. This was a fool's paradise, she told herself, but it didn't stop her savouring every moment of it.

Yet, as relentless as the sands of time, the end had to come.

And come it did.

As was their custom most evenings after the evening meal, they were sitting on the verandah, enjoying the peace at the close of the day. The air was completely still, not even the slightest waft of breeze. The landscape was drenched in the light of a full moon. No clouds. There hadn't been clouds for years. It didn't seem the drought would ever break. Rebecca looked at the excavated dam. Right now it was a stark wound in the ground, waiting for the water that would give it life. But one day...

Slade shifted restlessly in the wicker armchair that had been her grandfather's. He pushed himself out of it and stepped to the edge of the verandah. His head tilted as he stared up at the stars, a vast panoply of stars that shone more brilliantly in the outback than anywhere else in the world, as if the silence and lonely vastness of the land drew them closer, whispering the age-old message that this earth was part of them, part of the cycle of the whole universe.

The words that broke the silence were quietly spoken, but they not only shattered the peace of the evening, they also heralded in the hard inexorable reality that Rebecca had always known she would have to face.

"I have to go away, at least for a few days," Slade said, then turned to her, gesturing an apologetic appeal. "It's something I have to handle personally, Rebecca. If I could delegate it, I would. But I can't."

Rebecca sat very still, feeling a coldness creep through her body, a terrible tightness creep over her face. She had to force out the words that her lips didn't want to say. "You can come and go as you please, Slade. You don't have to consult with me. There's no obligation to—"

He muttered some savage imprecation under his breath, then threw his hands up in exasperated appeal. "We've been together for nearly a month and you can still say that? What do I have to do to get through to you, Rebecca? It's not that I want to go."

He dropped his hands, shook his head and paced the verandah, pausing to shake his head again before swinging around to come back to her.

Rebecca watched the very deliberate air of his approach in bleak resignation, knowing this was the beginning of the end. Brisbane. Then back to New York. He would go because he had to go—there was no one else to take on his responsibilities—and then there would be pressures on him to stay longer than he meant to; he wouldn't be able to get away. He had probably neglected things to remain with her this long, creating problems that would require all the more of his attention when he was faced with them.

"Ever since we met I seem to have been fighting rejection from you, Rebecca," he threw at her with a violent edge of frustration. "You look on me as though I'm some temporary lover who can't be trusted with your full confidence. It doesn't seem to matter what I do or say. So why don't you give me the answer? How do I get you to believe in me?"

The idea came impulsively to Rebecca as she looked into his grimly determined face. At least it would guarantee that she would have him near her when she needed him most.

"There is something you can do, Slade," she said quickly before she could have second thoughts.

"Tell me!" he urged, his eyes glittering with a deep inner impatience.

"You can make the time to be with me when I give birth to our baby."

It was a purely rational challenge. If Slade truly wanted to share in her life and in their child's life, if he was deepdown genuine and this was not a passing impulse, a *novelty* that would eventually get buried under the weight of his other life, then one way or another he would make a point of being with her at the birth of their child.

"Of course I'll be with you!" he assured her. "I'll take you to the hospital, stay by your side the whole time. I want to be there, Rebecca."

She shook her head. "No hospital, Slade. This baby is going to be born on Wildjanna, just as I was, and my father and uncle and brother whose graves are also here at Wildjanna. This will be the fourth generation and I'm not going to any hospital."

He stared at her in total disbelief. "Rebecca, you can't be serious!"

"Never more so," she returned coolly.

The disbelief slowly changed to a look of appalled contemplation. "You have to have a doctor in attendance. You can't...you can't just have a baby by yourself," he protested.

"I'll call the Flying Doctor Service. Unless there's some known medical reason against it, most babies are born on the home properties out here, Slade," she explained.

"What if the doctor can't get here in time," he argued frantically. "What if..." He had gone white in the face. He swallowed convulsively. "I have no experience in this kind of thing, Rebecca!" His eyes wildly challenged hers. "What if I'm away when it...when it starts happening...and the doctor can't come?"

Excuses, she thought, and dropped her gaze from his. She looked out over Wildjanna, her facade of calm composure hiding the painful pounding of her heart. "Nature does most of the work," she said tonelessly. "I'll manage by myself if I have to. You please yourself what you do, Slade. It doesn't worry me."

"Rebecca, I am coming back." There was a thread of desperation in the harshness of his voice. "It's just for a few days."

"Of course," she agreed, keeping her eyes fixed on the landscape. She gave a little shrug. "Whatever you want, Slade."

"I'll bring you back an architect. A builder. An interior decorator."

She looked at him as though he had taken leave of his senses. "What do you imagine I want them for?"

"To check over the additions to the house for the children's project," he replied with an air of triumphant satisfaction. "You want to get started on it, don't you?"

She had discussed her plans with several authorities and they had been met with co-operative appreciation. However, it had been pointed out that special amenities would have to be provided for children whose failing health could not bear any stress. The additions meant some structural changes to the homestead.

Rebecca had shown Slade the plans she had drawn up. He had examined them with interest, and made a couple of suggestions, which she had noted down. The topic hadn't been fully pursued because Slade had started playing with her hair and that had led to other things.

"I can't afford to build right now," she said decisively. "Once the drought breaks I'll be able to start thinking about it."

"I told you that Cordell Enterprises would supply the funds to do whatever was required. There's no need to wait," Slade argued.

Rebecca frowned at him. "Slade, I feel you're trying to buy me. This is my home. Whatever needs to be done to it, I'll do. The travelling costs and any medical equipment—

that's different. I won't accept your paying out any money for additions to my home, Slade."

"It's not for you! It's for the children!" he retorted vehemently. "Besides, I intend to make this my home, too. If you have some objection to that, you'd better state it now. Otherwise, I'm bringing an architect, a builder and an interior decorator back with me."

He was right. She shouldn't let her pride delay anything when that meant depriving some children of what Wildjanna could give them. And she certainly had no objection to Slade making his home here whenever he could.

"Okay," she agreed. "Bring back whomever you want."

Slade heaved a sigh of relief. His voice dropped to a soft persuasive note. "Rebecca, you don't really mean that about having the baby here."

"Yes, I do."

Her eyes flashed her determination at him. She wasn't going to let Slade buy her off with his help for her project. If he wanted to be counted, let him stand and be counted when it was most important to her, not when he could make some convenient time for dropping in on her life!

His head jerked away, then slowly turned back. "I'll call you every day. At five o'clock. And I'll want to know all you've been doing, to make sure you've not gone wild and done...the things you shouldn't. Five o'clock," he repeated as though impelled to stamp it into her mind.

"As you like," she said flatly. "I may or may not be here to take the call. It will depend on what I'm doing. I won't spend my life hanging on what you do, Slade."

"I want you in my life, Rebecca," he said fiercely.

She pushed herself out of her chair, ruing the undeniable fact that her body was no longer lithe or graceful. She was into her sixth month of pregnancy and although she was still in fairly trim shape, her balance was not as good as it normally was. Nevertheless, she threw her shoulders back and faced Slade with resolute pride.

"I made the baby. The rest of this situation was made by you, Slade. I didn't ask it of you. I can look after myself, and I want this baby too much to put its well-being at risk. Do what you have to do. I'm not stopping you."

Conflict warred across his face. "Whatever I have to do, whatever I have to accomplish, I'll win your love, Rebecca Wilder, if it's the last thing I ever do!" he declared vehemently.

It was the last thing she had ever expected to hear from Slade, and for a moment Rebecca was too stunned to make any reply to it. Desire, yes. The will to have his own way, yes. But to want her love.... He hadn't even believed in love. Did this mean he loved her?

"I hope so, Slade. I truly hope so," she said in a voice that shook with turbulent emotion, hopelessly aware that she already loved him.

Unaccountably tears pricked her eyes and she turned aside, not wanting Slade to misinterpret them as distress at his going. He caught her, his arms sliding over the tight bulge of the baby and gently pulling her against the vibrant tautness of his body. His warm mouth moved seductively over her ear. "I'll tame you yet," he murmured huskily.

"Do you really want me to be tamed, Slade?" she whispered, then swivelled in his embrace and kissed him with all the fierce passion that he aroused in her.

There was no more talking that night.

Slade left the next day.

A call came from him every afternoon at five o'clock. Although Rebecca berated herself for her growing dependency on that link with him, she could not deny herself the pleasure of some communication, however unsatisfied it left her.

There were seven long days before Slade returned to Wildjanna. With an architect and a builder and an interior decorator. Rebecca's reunion with Slade was constrained by the presence of the three visitors who had to be given most of her attention. They spent the rest of the day taking a lot of measurements and consulting with Rebecca, making sure they knew all her requirements and the requirements of the job. Rebecca readily agreed with the arrangements Slade had made for work to begin as soon as possible, and by the time all three flew off again in the plane, late in the afternoon, this part of the project was completely in their very capable hands.

"Satisfied?" Slade asked when they were gone.

"Yes, thank you," Rebecca returned lightly, unsure what Slade wanted from her.

There was a tense portending air about him, which stayed with him indefinitely, as though he was waiting for something to happen. Strangely enough, Rebecca had the impression that it was not entirely focused on her, yet she was mixed up in it. She wondered if she was supposed to express gladness that he was with her again, or if he expected her to give in and say she would marry him after all.

She did neither.

Her gladness was obvious anyway, and she was determined not to use any emotional pressure on him or take any from him. Their relationship could not survive that kind of strain. Unless they respected each other's rights to carry on their separate lives, the situation would fast become utterly destructive.

As it was, Rebecca couldn't see it lasting. Which was why a marriage between them couldn't even be contemplated. This minor separation would inevitably be followed by others, and once the baby was born, they would probably become longer and longer. If they married, the time would eventually come when they spent so little of their lives together that divorce was a foregone conclusion. And then if Slade decided to fight her for their child . . .

"No commitment unless it was a forever commitment," Rebecca recited firmly to herself, but as it turned out, Slade didn't press her for anything. They resumed their daily routine at Wildjanna as though he had never been away, as though nothing had changed at all. Except something had. Rebecca could not shake off the feeling that Slade was waiting for something.

It was almost two weeks before she found out what it was, and even when the first intimation came, she didn't realise what it meant. They had just finished dinner one night when Milly came hurrying into the dining-room, her face reflecting a conflict of interests as she darted anxious looks at both Slade and Rebecca before announcing that Rebecca was wanted in the office.

"What for?" Rebecca asked.

Milly hesitated, her answer curiously circumspect. "There's a call for you. You have to take it."

"Who is it?" Rebecca demanded, slowly pushing herself up from the table.

Milly looked pained. She darted another anxious look at Slade. "Mr. Neilsen," she gabbled quickly.

Rebecca's heart leapt in shock. "Paul? Paul is calling me?"

Rebecca raced for the office, her mind awhirl with disturbing possibilities. In the almost four years since the accident Paul had never made contact with her at Wildjanna. It had always been she who had called or visited him. Something must have happened to him, she thought, fighting down a sense of panic. He must need her.

She grabbed the receiver and lowered herself shakily into the chair in front of it. She forced herself to take a deep breath, afraid that her voice would be trembling like the rest of her. She owed Paul Neilsen her life. Anything he wanted of her she had to give.

"Paul? It's Rebecca," she announced as steadily as she could.

"I hope I haven't called you away from anything important, Rebecca." His voice sounded calm and warmly friendly.

"Not at all," she affirmed quickly, then not believing there could be no particular import behind this extraordinary event, she pressed, "How are you?"

"Fine! Very happy!" he said, a little too heartily to Rebecca's ear. "I wanted you to be the first to hear my news, Rebecca. We've shared so much together, been friends for so long—" the heartiness cracked a little. She heard a swift intake of breath. "And I know you'll want to wish me every happiness in my life, just as I wish you every happiness in yours. I'm getting married, Rebecca."

Married! Paul getting married to someone else! The shock of it left her speechless.

"Her name is Susan Hanley," Paul's voice continued brightly. "She's a wonderful person. She's been working for me for over a year now." He gave a forced little laugh. "She even anticipates my needs before I think of them."

Someone else fulfilling his needs as she had once fulfilled them before the accident. Paul had never loved her. Rebecca suddenly knew that beyond any doubt now. When the fantasy of running Wildjanna with her had come crashing down, he hadn't wanted the commitment of the marriage they had planned.

Paul's choice.

Slade's words came back to her, slowly relieving her of the long hangover of guilt over Paul's injuries. She was still grateful to Paul for saving her life, but the burden that had placed on her heart was no longer a heavy one. He had found a woman who suited him better, a woman he wanted to marry.

"When are you getting married?" she asked, pushing a brittle brightness into her voice. Paul had known this Susan Hanley for a year, a whole year. No wonder he had looked so anguished when she had begged him to marry her at the airport that day. He was embarrassed even now. She could tell from the forced cheerfulness in his voice.

"Tomorrow."

She weathered this shock a little more cynically. Paul had put off telling her the truth until the last moment. Did he think she would make a scene? Another impassioned plea for him to change his mind? She supposed she couldn't blame him for thinking that. She had clung on so long. But he could have been more honest with her. All these years he had let her think his disaffection was because of his disabilities from the accident. Had he pitied her for clinging to a dream that he knew was over?

"I hope the sun shines for you, for you and your bride, tomorrow and always," she said, trying her best to demonstrate there was no ill will on her part. What they had had together was well and truly over. It had only ever been an illusion anyway. She truly hoped that Paul loved his Susan.

"Thank you, Rebecca." There was relief in his voice. "And I hope it rains for Wildjanna very soon."

"Yes. We sorely need it. Thank you for calling, Paul. I do wish you, both of you, every happiness."

"And I you," he added softly. "In your future life. Goodbye, Rebecca."

The finality in his voice was unmistakable.

"Goodbye," she echoed.

She heard the line disconnect and knew the last line had been spoken between them. There had been no suggestion that they could all be friends. That chapter of their lives was definitely closed. And in truth, Rebecca was content for it to be so. She wished she could see her future with Slade as clearly as Paul could see his with Susan Hanley.

Married . . . tomorrow.

Tears blurred her eyes and she hastily blinked them away. It was weak to cry. She had made her choice with Slade, and half a loaf with him was better than nothing at all. Besides, she would soon have the baby. Her hand went to her swollen tummy, gently caressing the mound of her child . . . Slade's child. She would always have some part of him, no matter what else the future held.

She didn't know how she knew that Slade was near, watching her, waiting. Some sixth sense picked up the force field of his presence. She looked around and he was there in the office doorway, grim-faced and emanating so much tension that Rebecca felt choked by it.

He didn't ask any questions. He didn't say a word. It came to her in a lightning flash of intuition that Slade knew what Paul's call had been about, not only knew but had known before she did. It was Paul's call that he had been waiting for ever since he had returned from Brisbane.

"You had something to do with this, Slade?" she asked, wanting to know precisely what he had done.

"Yes," he replied unashamedly. "I went to see him. You now know that he's never going to marry you. Never, Rebecca," he repeated, his face stamped with ruthless purpose.

What a strange meeting that must have been, she mused. The blackest of black comedies. Slade believing she still loved Paul. Paul believing the same. Both of them wanting the final severance of a relationship that didn't suit either of them. Poor Rebecca, they would have thought. But necessary to be cruel to be kind.

It was humiliating to think of them discussing her like that behind her back. Pride stirred. She didn't need them to decide her life for her. She could stand alone if she had to. If Slade thought this would change the situation between them, he was badly mistaken.

Her green eyes flashed steely determination at him. "That doesn't mean I'll marry you, Slade," she stated flatly.

A savagely determined glitter leapt into the vivid blue eyes. "Right now, I'll settle for something else. But we're going to make a family—you and I and our child, Rebecca. And one by one, I'm going to hack away all your restraints from marrying me until you're left with no other choice. Then you're going to love *me*. Not him."

In that moment he wore the relentless air of a conqueror who recognised no barriers, and Rebecca felt her will crumbling under the strength of it. There was a stirring of response deep within her, a strange wanting to be his conquest, whatever the cost. Did he love her, she wondered? Or was this simply his need to possess, to stamp his domination on whatever he wanted, to win his way?

Rebecca didn't like to think of herself as a conquest. It was an alien feeling to everything she had ever lived by. Her destiny was her own to carve, not to be bent to Slade Cordell's will. She wanted a partnership, a mating for life. No way would she be Slade's woman unless he was her man...permanently.

"You can't make me marry you, Slade," she said quietly.

"I'll make it possible." His voice softened as he continued, becoming more appealing. "Your life and Paul Neilsen's crossed for a time. That time is over, Rebecca. Now it's our lives that are together. Paul recognised that immediately."

Her mouth curled in savage irony. "Yes. I imagine he did. With you telling him so, Slade."

He didn't so much as flinch. His eyes bored steadily into hers. "He doesn't love you, Rebecca."

She didn't flinch, either. "I know."

"He didn't want to share his life with you."

She shrugged and turned away. "I made a mistake," she said flatly. "Maybe I'm making another mistake with you."

"No!" He was across the room in a few swift strides, pulling her up from her chair, enfolding her in a tight embrace. She couldn't find the strength to resist. She sagged against the rocklike indomitability of his body and was soothed by his sharing it with her. She didn't want to be alone.

"This is our time, Rebecca," Slade insisted passionately, then kissed her with a driven need to impress that on her, to impress himself on her.

Rebecca didn't fight it.

She was content for it to be so.

For as long as it lasted.

But she would not marry him.

Apart from her own need to keep Slade's child, she had to safeguard the fourth generation for Wildjanna.

CHAPTER THIRTEEN

IT SEEMED a strange contradiction to Rebecca that although she and Slade spent less time with each other over the next two months, they grew closer together. Slade ritually went missing for at least two days a week, often at the weekends, flying off to Brisbane to deal with whatever business demanded his attention. He never failed to call her every evening he was away, and Rebecca was never left in any doubt that he would soon be with her at Wildjanna again.

She didn't mind these absences. Slade had to be free to do what he wanted, as she was to do as she wanted. The rapidly advancing state of her pregnancy meant that she had to leave most of the station work to the stock men, who readily carried out her instructions. Or Slade's, if he rode out with them, which he often did when he was home.

Slade invariably called Wildjanna home. He would get off the plane from his trips to Brisbane, give her a huge grin, sweep her into his arms and with a sigh of deep contentment breathe, "It's good to be home again." It was impossible to disbelieve him. Rebecca still refused to look too far ahead, but her own happiness in their relationship could not be denied.

Slade's pleasure in sharing everything he could with her deepened Rebecca's pleasure in his company. Work had begun on the additions to the homestead so she was not at all bored or frustrated from being restricted in the more physical work of the cattle station. Not only did she supervise every step of what was being done to her home, but there was a battery of correspondence to carry through, with letters to and from hospitals and the societies that dealt with the children who concerned her. Because of Slade's help, the project could be brought forward to almost a standby footing.

As soon as the baby was born and she was back to full working capacity, Rebecca intended to begin. If only the drought would break, everything would be perfect. It would be even more perfect if Slade could stay with her forever.

She had thought he might find her less and less desirable as her body swelled into an unlovely and cumbersome shape. However, far from being put off from the more intimate side of their life, Slade seemed to adore every aspect of her pregnancy.

Rebecca wondered if it was because this was a completely new experience for him. Another *novelty*. Yet he made her feel so loved and cherished that she didn't care why he did it, as long as he kept doing it.

He brought home bottles of beautifully scented body oil, which he gently rubbed into her tightly stretched abdomen. His eyes always reflected an awed delight if the baby moved while he was doing this. He made love more gently as time went on, mostly taking and giving a deep wondrous satisfaction in cradling her body spoon fashion against his, and embracing their child as well as Rebecca in their total intimacy.

He brought her books on prenatal care and insisted she practise breathing and relaxation exercises. After several weeks of determined coaching for the birth process, Slade finally broached the critical subject of the baby's delivery.

"First babies can be difficult, Rebecca," he warned her, clearly having done quite a bit of reading on it himself. "I know you have no fears about it, and you think it's all very natural, but you haven't had the experience and..."

He took a deep breath, his eyes pleading with hers in deep concern. "Please rethink about going into a hospital for the delivery. I promise you I'll be with you every minute. It's not that I want to shirk any responsibility. I just don't want anything to go wrong, either for you or the baby."

He was so deeply disturbed about it that Rebecca hesitated only a few moments before giving in. Although it meant their child would not be born on Wildjanna, Slade had given her so much that she could not feel it was fair to ignore his fears. The important thing was that their child be born safely, and she had no doubt that Slade would be with her.

In fact, she was almost ready to change her mind about marrying him. If he still wanted her to, after the baby was born, Rebecca was considering it. She was almost sure Slade would never intentionally do anything to hurt her. If he would agree to leave their child with her on Wildjanna—it seemed he might be content to do that, coming back to them whenever he could.

"All right. I'll go to hospital when the baby's due," she promised him.

"I'll make all the arrangements," he said in a happy burst of relief. "You won't have to worry about a thing, Rebecca. I'll take care of every possible contingency."

She accompanied Slade on his next trip to Brisbane and had a thorough medical checkup. The doctor declared that everything was coming along just fine, which was what Rebecca had confidently expected, but it seemed to set Slade's mind at rest.

They had a buying spree for all the baby's needs and ended up with twice as much as was necessary. Slade just couldn't contain himself, and it was such a joyful exciting outing together that Rebecca didn't have the heart to chide him for his extravagance.

He went completely wild in a soft toy department, ending up with an armful of adorable furry animals, some of which played nursery tunes, and when they returned to their hotel he lined them all up and sat listening to them with such a fatuous grin on his face that Rebecca couldn't help laughing at him. And loving him.

There was, however, one contingency over which Slade had no power, a contingency that the land had thirsted for throughout five long parched years. Rebecca's pregnancy was three weeks short of its full term when the clouds at last began to gather, huge black clouds that rolled over the sky, blotting out a sun that had ruled without pity for far too long. And the rain, the blessed life-giving rain, began to fall.

It started as a gentle sprinkle but did not remain that way for very long. Nor did the brief teasing shower that followed. It soon developed into a teeming downpour that beat at the ground, demanding entry. The dust was settled. Cracks in the earth swallowed their fill and closed. The water began running over the land, into the creek, into the new dam below the homestead. All the station hands on Wildjanna danced out in the pounding downpour and whooped for joy, soaked to the skin and loving every minute of it.

Any rainfall was good, but Rebecca prayed that this was not simply a passing storm. They needed days of rain before it could be confidently said that the drought was broken. By nightfall several inches had been measured and there was no easing of the torrential downpour. News reports on the radio stated that rain was sweeping right across central Australia. Some areas were already reporting flash flooding, and the drought was certainly eased, if not ended. The weather forecast for the following day was for more and heavier rain.

Rebecca and Slade lay awake in their bed for a long time, listening to the thundering beat of it on the iron roof. It was music to Rebecca's ears.

"I've never seen or heard anything like this," Slade remarked in wondering awe.

Rebecca laughed and snuggled up to him. "The outback is a land of primitive extremes, Slade. Nothing ever comes in half measures. Drought, flood, fire…most times, all you can do is fight to survive the worst, then ride the crest of the best. It's both humbling and exhilarating, but always there is the challenge to keep pace with it. There's a harmony that has to be maintained, a link…" She heaved a deep sigh. "I don't know how to describe it."

"Elemental," Slade said, then grinned at her look of surprise. "I am not the blind city boy you think I am."

"No, you're not," she agreed, and sighed in contentment as his arm tightened around her.

She must have fallen asleep in an awkward position because the next morning Rebecca woke with a dragging ache in her lower back. Nevertheless, the nagging discomfort was quickly overridden by the excitement of hearing the rain still falling. Bubbling with high spirits, Rebecca pushed herself out of bed, dragged on a gown and hurried out to walk around the verandah and see how much change there had been during the night.

The new dam was already halfway to becoming a lake. The creek was rising fast and the ground was turning into a quagmire of squelching mud. It was a beautiful sight to Rebecca. As Slade joined her and slid an arm around her shoulders, she looked at him with sparkling eyes.

"I'm afraid you're not going to be able to get to Brisbane this week, Slade," she declared, smugly pleased that he would be forced to stay with her. "We'll be bogged in for quite a few days. No plane can come in or take off in these conditions.''

''I didn't intend to go anyway,'' he returned with a funny little smile.

''No more problems for a while?'' she asked lightly, hoping that would be the case until after the baby was born.

''Not for me.''

The note of finality in his voice stirred her curiosity. She had made it a rule never to ask about his business, wary of being tempted to make demands that she had no right to make, but now she recalled that he hadn't spent any time at all in his office since his last trip away.

''Are you taking a vacation?'' she asked, wanting to know how long this situation would last.

He met her eyes with a look of searching intensity, as though wary of her response to the answer of the question. ''Something like that,'' was his rather obscure reply.

Rebecca was unsure whether to pursue the point or not. She was still hesitating over it when Milly called out that a news broadcast on the radio had said that the Diamantina River was in full spate. Rebecca's mind instantly turned to more urgent matters. The stock on Wildjanna had to be herded to high ground.

''If it floods, the Diamantina spills to a great lake, ninety miles across,'' she explained to Slade. ''Windy Drop-Down Creek is a tributary. We've got to be prepared.''

Slade frowned, then gave a slight shake of his head. ''You mean ninety yards across, don't you? Not even the Amazon River...''

''No, Slade. I don't know about the Amazon, but in a big wet, the Diamantina has been up to ninety miles wide.'' Her eyes danced at him as he shook his head again, not in disbelief, but in a bemused reaction to coming to grips with the realities of the outback. "You'll see it for yourself if the rain keeps up," Rebecca assured him.

"Ninety miles," he muttered. "No half measures about that!"

Slade immediately got ready to ride out with the stock men, assuring her he would look after everything and see that the cattle were moved to higher ground. Rebecca watched him go from the homestead verandah, wishing she could go with him, but consoled by her pleasure in knowing that the drought really was ending.

So much had happened throughout its five-year course— Pa's death, Paul's terrible accident, the fateful meeting with Slade, which would never have occurred but for the necessity to conserve water, and then Gran's death and her own decision to have Slade's child. A new life, she thought happily, everywhere a new life. After the rain came the regrowth, losses to be recovered, breeding programs to be initiated, a replenishing of the continuing cycle of nature.

Emilio Dalvarez would come flying back from Argentina, Rebecca thought with an indulgent sense of affection. He had always been a good neighbour and she could no longer hold any grudge about his interference in her personal affairs. Emilio had probably meant well, and his visit to New York had resulted in Slade coming to her a month earlier than he had planned.

She remembered her own visit to New York, the crossing point in hers and Slade's so vastly separate lifelines, and shook her head in bemusement over all that had eventuated from it. Slade had not concerned himself with the management of Devil's Elbow since then. There had been no need. They were running both properties as one, and now the rain would answer any problems that might have arisen.

Rebecca grew more conscious of the ache in her lower back as the morning wore on, but she attached no significance to it. The first rolling wave of pain came a couple of hours after lunch. It was not sharp enough to unduly disturb her. She had read that from the seventh month of pregnancy onwards it was not unusual to feel practice contractions. However, the second one, only an hour later, gave her pause for thought.

It couldn't be, Rebecca decided. There were still three weeks, almost three weeks, to go, and she wasn't ready to have the baby yet. Besides, with the rain coming down like this, she couldn't get to the hospital. A couple of pains were just a couple of pains, nothing to get in a fuss about. She was a normal, healthy person. There was no reason at all for her to give birth prematurely. Nevertheless, the nagging ache in her back was ominously constant. Rebecca checked the time, just in case she should.

Sure enough, almost to the hour, another pain rolled through her, lasting about thirty seconds. It was really happening, Rebecca thought in dazed wonderment. The baby wanted to be born. He or she was not content to wait for the normal timetable. Rebecca had to fight off a wild surge of excitement and force her mind to work along practical lines.

She had promised Slade that she would go to hospital for the delivery. A plane was out of the question, but a helicopter could lift her from Wildjanna. Slade wouldn't care how much it cost. She went into the office to make the necessary calls, then realised that even if there was a procurable helicopter, it couldn't get to Wildjanna before darkness fell. The weather conditions were hazardous for even daylight hours.

Nevertheless, she had to follow Slade's wishes. She called the Flying Doctor Service, informed them of her condition and asked for advice. The best they could do was to have a doctor on standby to give instructions should the birth occur during the night. Their information was that all air-rescue helicopters were out on missions to pick up people in danger of being drowned in the flooding. Rebecca made several more calls but they only served to confirm what she had already surmised. An imminent birth was not as critical as an imminent death, and she had no hope of being picked up before morning.

She bent over as another contraction made itself felt, automatically employing the breathing technique that would minimise the discomfort. The office clock confirmed that the time elapsed from the last one was only forty-five minutes. Rebecca figured the baby was following its own schedule and was not about to wait on anyone's convenience. Maybe it wanted to be born on Wildjanna. Maybe it knew it was the fourth generation.

The thought brought a blissful smile to Rebecca's lips as she hugged her cumbersome body. *It will be all right,* she told her baby. *I know what you're doing and I'm going to help you all the way.*

Slade got back to the homestead just at dusk. He came in wet and muddy but spreading cheer with the news that the cattle had all been herded onto high ground. He seemed enormously satisfied with his day's work, and grinned happily as he recalled that he didn't have to stint on water tonight. He was going to soak in a full hot bath for at least an hour, and Rebecca could reward him for his labours by soaping his back.

Rebecca suppressed her own news until he was stretched out in steaming water and thoroughly relaxed. "I've been labouring, too," she said, her eyes dancing with her inner knowledge as she lathered soap over his chest.

"Mmm..." It was half a question, half a sound of sensual pleasure.

"Our child is on its way into the world."

Slade's eyes flew open. His body jackknifed into a sitting position. "Rebecca, you don't mean now!"

She nodded, then quickly explained that there was no way she could get to hospital in time for the delivery—she had tried—and they would have to manage the birth themselves.

Slade fought the waves of panic that pummelled his stomach and made a useless mash of his mind. Rebecca had no fear. He must not show fear. He recited that thought over and over in chaotic desperation. His worst nightmare was coming true, but showing fear was the worst possible thing he could do. He was not going to fail her. He was going to make her believe in him. And please God, he prayed wildly, don't let anything go wrong.

The host of expressions that flitted across Slade's face went too fast for Rebecca to identify, but it was determination that finally settled on it. "I can do it, Rebecca. You're not to worry or be afraid. I can do it," he assured her. "I've got everything we need stored away in my office. Have you told Milly?"

"Not yet. I didn't want to panic her."

"I'll need her help. But you're not to worry. I'll explain it all to Milly and get her organised."

Rebecca shook her head in bewilderment. "What have you got stored away in your office?"

"The midwife equipment." He surged out of the bath and started drying himself, all his movements brisk and purposeful. *It's just a case of mind over matter,* he told himself. Hadn't he always prided himself on his competence? A little baby wasn't going to beat him. *Except it's my baby,* his mind screamed. *Rebecca's and mine! And everything's got to go right!*

Rebecca stared at him in sheer astonishment. "How do you come to have midwife equipment?"

He gave her a rueful smile. "I learnt how to do it in case something like this happened. I said I'd look after you, Rebecca, and I will. I've done a midwifery course, watched deliveries . . ."

"But you said I had to go to hospital!"

He sighed. "Rebecca, the more you learn, the more you become aware of what can go wrong. It's not much of a risk. Most deliveries are straightforward. So you're not to worry. I can handle it," he insisted earnestly.

Another pain surged through Rebecca, putting reality ahead of theory. Slade instantly sprang into action, gently rubbing her lower back as he coached her breathing.

"How long since the last one?" he asked when the pain had receded.

"About forty minutes."

"Okay. Try to relax now. We'll go and tell Milly and start getting prepared."

Apart from the few contractions, which required her complete concentration, Rebecca was in a constant state of amazement over the next two hours. Slade had Milly so busy sterilising basins and preparing one of the bedrooms that the housekeeper quickly recovered from her initial shock over the news and did his bidding with an air of incredulous fascination. Which echoed Rebecca's own feelings.

Slade might well have been a doctor himself, he was so knowing and confident and meticulous in his preparations. Everything was accomplished with a calm efficiency that inspired the utmost confidence in his claim that he knew all about handling a home delivery.

Rebecca was both mortified by the lack of faith she had once shown in him and exalted that he had gone so far to prove that she could trust him and depend on him. Few husbands would do so much for their wives, and she had refused to marry him, not only refused, but couched her rejection of him in the bitterest terms by comparing him to Paul.

Slade was a far finer man than Paul, far stronger, far more caring about her needs, far more loving. Shame burned through Rebecca, such deep shame that she felt driven to confess the truth of her feelings for him. She hadn't been fair to Slade. She hadn't been fair at all.

"I thought you went to Brisbane on business," she began, pained now by the reservations she had kept harbouring, the reservations that had forced Slade to such lengths in order to prove she could trust him. "I had no idea you would... would care so much. I just wanted you with me when the baby was born. I thought Cordell Enterprises would take you away from me and—"

"It never will, Rebecca," Slade said, his eyes gravely promising that truth. "Believe me, this means more to me than anything else in my whole life."

"I believe you," she whispered, her own eyes filling with emotional tears. "Having you with me... it means a lot to me, too, Slade. More—more than I can ever say. And doing all this for me..."

"Lucky I did. I'm not sure how well I would have coped otherwise." He gently wiped away the spill of tears on her cheeks. "You're doing fine," he said softly. "Just think about having the baby, Rebecca. We made it together and we're going to bring it into the world together. Okay?"

She nodded and quickly sucked in her breath as another pain started. He was so good to her during each contraction, encouraging her to lean on him or take up any position she found most comfortable for riding it through. She didn't want to lie down. Milly brought her drinks when her mouth and lips got dry from all the shallow breathing. Slade held her hand and told her heartwarming stories about the births he had witnessed during his midwife course.

The time between the contractions kept lessening and the pain grew progressively stronger. By midnight they were only five minutes apart, barely enough pause to recover from one before the next started. Rebecca had to lie down.

Milly sat on the chair beside the bed and held Rebecca's hand tight while Slade carried out a full examination. He reported that the baby was in the right birth position. Everything was going by the textbook, Slade assured himself, but textbook data—not even the few deliveries he had seen were anything as harrowing as this.

He felt utterly helpless, trapped within a situation over which he had no real control, unable to take Rebecca's pain upon himself, unable to make the baby come faster. The only relief was in knowing that everything was normal. So far. If anything started to go wrong... But he had to keep thinking positive, help Rebecca, make it right!

The next half-hour was wave after wave of continual agony. Rebecca coped as well as she could but she couldn't help crying out. Slade grew so distressed he wanted to give her an injection, but Rebecca refused to have it, insisting that she wasn't going to interfere with the natural process in any way. Slade helped her onto the pillows and lifted her knees up, sure that she was about to move into the second stage of labour, and no sooner did he have her positioned than the membranes ruptured and she had a blessed feeling of release as the forewaters flooded down.

"Okay, Rebecca, we're ready to move," Slade told her, trying his utmost to keep his voice steady and all that he had learnt clear in his head. "When you feel the urge to push, push," he instructed. "Go with the contraction. Don't fight it. And don't panic."

"Won't panic," she gasped as the compulsion to bear down began.

There was a terrible maelstrom of panic circling Slade's mind but he refused to let it in. Rebecca had suffered so much. He was not going to fail her when she needed him most. He was not going to fail her!

The pushing part was not so bad, but the pain in between had Rebecca breathing hard. Slade kept encouraging her, telling her that everything was going fine. The steady conviction in his eyes helped. Her eyes clung trustingly to that conviction. Slade wouldn't let her down, she thought. He had never let her down. He had done all he said he would do, and now he was standing by her in her hour of need. Standing by her as few men would or could. So strong. So steadfast. Looking after her. Loving her. He had to love her. No man would do all this for her unless he loved her.

"You're doing great! Just one or two more pushes, Rebecca," Slade soothed. *I'm ready,* he told himself. *I'm ready to do all I have to do to make sure our baby is born safely. Only another few minutes. My hands are shaking. I've got to stop my hands from shaking. Concentrate...*

"Milly, hold the cleaning towel and bunny rug ready," he commanded.

Rebecca pushed.

"The head is coming now," Slade cried excitedly. The miracle of it...a beautiful, perfect head. He had it in his hands. Their child... "Keep pushing, Rebecca. Shoulders..."

She felt a slithering release accompanied by more water, then heard her baby's first cry. What a wonderful sound it was!

"My child..." The awe and wonder in Slade's voice billowed through Rebecca's mind.

"Is it a boy or girl?" she asked, too exhausted to move but so exhilarated she wanted to do so much more. She wanted to feel her baby, touch it tenderly.

"Rebecca, I reckon you've just given birth to the first female president of the United States." Slade's voice was bursting with relief and pride and joy as he quickly placed his child—her child—over Rebecca's stomach, her head hanging down over Rebecca's waist to stop her from inhaling any fluid. "Or, if not that," he raved on, grabbing the cleaning towel from Milly to wipe the wetness from the tiny body, "I guess she'll make the finest astrophysicist in the whole world."

He'd done it! He'd done it right! Their daughter was safe and sound! Born to them this night—born to both of them—they'd made her together and brought her into the world together, their very own child, alive, healthy, perfect! It had been the most frightening experience of his life, but the reward, the ultimate reward of it, a new life! Thank you, God! If You're out there watching over us, thank you... thank you... for this new life!

"I think you're forgetting Wildjanna," Rebecca said indulgently, her eyes feasting on the unbelievable perfection of their baby.

"Never," Slade said with deep conviction. "Wildjanna is her home. It will always be her home, no matter where she goes or what she does."

The fourth generation.

Are you looking down from somewhere, Gran? Rebecca thought wistfully. Do you know I've kept the faith that you and Pa brought to this land we call home? This is your bloodline, mine, fathered by a man who is strong enough to stand beside me, Gran. The mission to New York, your last command, it took me to him, brought him to me... and now the line will go on with this child who was born on Wildjanna tonight.

Slade passed Milly the cleaning towel, took the bunny rug, then with tender loving care wrapped his daughter up warmly and gently put her on Rebecca's breast. The feeling as her baby started sucking was unbelievable. She was so tiny, so beautiful... Rebecca cradled her in her arms and looked at Slade with blissful tears in her eyes.

"Thank you... thank you," she whispered.

It was all she could think of to say. She saw that there were tears in his eyes, too, and when he bent and kissed her, her heart was so full she thought it would burst with love.

"Got to clamp the cord now," he said huskily, and set about doing so. There was more to do, more to get right. He had to look after Rebecca, make sure he didn't forget anything. She was depending on him. She believed in him.

"What time is it?" she asked.

"Five past two," Milly answered, her voice uncharacteristically indulgent.

With an overwhelming sense of relief Slade followed through each step that completed the birth process, knowing that nothing, nothing at all had gone wrong. He couldn't stop smiling at Rebecca. She looked as though she was lost in a beautiful dream, looking down at their child at her breast. A couple of times Slade had to blink back tears. A grown man crying... It was absurd, yet surely there was nothing in the whole world—the whole universe—that could match the miracle of birth. And to see Rebecca like this... with their baby.

Time had lost all meaning for Rebecca. She had her long-awaited child, safe and sound in her arms. Then Slade brought in the baby's bath, and together they carefully washed their new little daughter and dressed her in the clothes they had bought.

The wonder of her choked both Slade and Rebecca into silence, but their daughter had no sense of awe at all. She loudly protested the whole bathing process, demonstrating a voice that was going to demand a lot of say in her life. But once she was snugly wrapped in a bunny rug again, she went straight to sleep.

The bassinet was ready for her, but Rebecca was loath to let her out of her embrace. Milly announced that she was off to bed. Her usually stoic face shone with warm benevolence as she dropped a kiss on Rebecca's forehead and ran a caressing finger down the baby's soft cheek. She gave Slade an approving nod, then left them alone together.

Rebecca smiled at Slade. "You must be tired, too."

He smiled back. "I'm too exhilarated to be tired."

"Yes. So am I." She shifted to the side of the bed. "Lie down with us, Slade. Hold me. Share her with me."

He heaved a deep sigh of contentment as he wrapped his arms around them both. Rebecca turned her head towards his and looked into his eyes, deep blue eyes that returned all that she felt. Perhaps even more.

"I've never loved anyone as much as I love you. And the child you've given me, Slade," she said softly. "If you still want me to marry you, I will."

"Rebecca..." He made her name sound like a long echoing dream of wanting and fulfilment. "I can't remember when I first knew I loved you. But this I know. You'll always have my love. As will our child, and any other children we have."

"Oh, Slade..." She was so choked with emotion she could barely speak.

He meant it. She knew he did. And she knew their lives were now irrevocably entwined. If Slade had to go away on business for Cordell Enterprises, it wouldn't change anything. The bond went too deep. Soul deep. They had made a family. She would never let anything destroy that. She would never let it be taken away from them.

CHAPTER FOURTEEN

NEITHER REBECCA NOR SLADE saw any necessity for her and the baby to be airlifted to a hospital. They both agreed that a medical checkup could be postponed until after the big wet. Slade informed the Flying Doctor Service that everything was fine and under control, mother and baby doing well.

The torrential rain eased off, but heavy showers continued to fall over the next ten days. The drought was well and truly ended. The dry red desert stirred from its long sleep and began to bloom, sprouting the green of fresh grasses. The great pendulum of life swung once more, transforming the landscape with vegetation that would be gradually consumed as the cycle moved on.

"In a few weeks, the plains will be covered in a riot of yellow daisies and purple parakeelya flowers," Rebecca informed Slade with shining eyes. "It's so stunningly beautiful..."

He chuckled. "I believe you. I'm starting to get used to all the surprises this land keeps dishing out to me." He shifted his gaze pointedly to the new lake where a black and white pageant of pelicans stretched around the far bank.

The previous morning they had been woken by the corellas' dawn chorus. A flock of galahs had swept in, their rich pink breasts rosier in the morning light, and two yellow-billed spoonbills had joined them, strutting a stately progress around the edge of the water, which reflected their white plumage.

"We'll be mobbed by budgerigars and zebra finches next." Rebecca laughed, then heaved a great sigh of satisfaction. "I'm so glad we excavated that dam. My only regret is that Gran isn't here to enjoy it."

Slade hugged her shoulders and dropped a kiss on her hair. "Her great-granddaughter is, and I reckon she'd be content with that."

Janet Logan Cordell, as she would be christened, suddenly decided she wasn't content, and gave a lusty yell to tell them she had woken up from her morning sleep and wanted to be lifted out of her lonely bassinet. Which Slade was only too happy to do. He was totally besotted with his baby daughter, who seemed to reciprocate the feeling. Any crying always ceased as soon as she was cradled against his broad shoulder. It was as though she instinctively knew that her father would make everything right for her. She hadn't yet learnt that not quite everything was within his power.

But Rebecca had been giving a lot of thought to that. She couldn't imagine that Slade could keep running Cordell Enterprises effectively from Brisbane. Sooner or later he would have to go back to New York and make his authority felt. The example of Devil's Elbow showed how management could get out of hand if it wasn't kept in check. Slade felt his responsibilities too deeply to let that happen again.

As much as Rebecca recoiled from the thought of living in New York, she figured she could stick it out without complaint for at least a month or two. She would have the baby to help keep her occupied while Slade was at work, and when they were all together...almost any sacrifice was worth that. It wasn't as if Slade would ever ask her to give up Wildjanna. She could always return when she wanted to, and Slade would come back to her as soon as he could.

He had done all the compromising in their relationship so
far. Not that he seemed at all unhappy about it. In fact,
there was no doubting his obvious contentment in their life
at Wildjanna. But as his wife—and she did want to be married to him, if only to confirm the sense of family for their
daughter—Rebecca felt it was only fair to offer Slade some
return for all his generosity.

They had decided to make a big day of their wedding at
Wildjanna. All the property owners in the Channel Country would be invited and they would make a triple celebra-
tion of the occasion, a marriage, a christening—both to be
performed by the flying padre who serviced the outback—
and a grand party to mark the end of the drought.

Slade was going to ask Emilio to be his best man. They
had received news that the Argentinian was on his way home
with a new wife, and Rebecca decided it would be a nice
welcoming gesture if she asked Emilio's bride to be matron
of honour. But that was all weeks ahead, when everything
had settled down after the rain and people could afford the
time away from their properties to relax and make merry.

Since Slade made no mention of having to leave Wildjanna before then, Rebecca assumed he had organised a
long vacation to cover their baby's birth. They were so
happy together it was all too easy for Rebecca to leave the
matter of her accompanying him to New York in abeyance.
That was a future thing that she would meet when they came
to it.

However, as it turned out, other circumstances prompted
her to tell Slade what she had decided. The rough clay air-
strip finally dried out enough for the mail plane to resume
its weekly drop at Wildjanna, and Slade eagerly raced off in
his Land Rover to meet it as it came in to land. He returned
with a bundle of letters and newspapers, which he handed
to Rebecca.

"There's something else, too," he informed her, with a great grin on his face. From the back of the vehicle he unloaded an old rocking chair, made of American oak and marked from many years of use. "It was Grandfather Logan's," Slade explained as he set it down on the verandah. "Just my size," he added as he settled into it and started it rocking. "I've been looking for a comfortable chair like this for quite some time."

That statement didn't make much sense to Rebecca but she couldn't help smiling at his smug air of satisfaction. "You had it brought all the way from America so you could rock here at your ease?" she laughingly teased.

"Grandfather Logan would approve. He was right all along. This will be the life for me," Slade declared.

"When you do have to go back to New York, I'll come with you, Slade," she said impulsively. "After all, our daughter should have a taste of your world, too. And besides, we both want to be with you."

The chair stopped rocking. The vivid blue eyes locked onto Rebecca's with an expression she couldn't read, but it made her heart flutter with gladness that she had made the offer. He came out of the chair slowly, took the bundle of mail from her hands and set it on the wicker table. Then he drew her into a gentle embrace and spoke in a voice that throbbed with deep emotion.

"Thank you, Rebecca. I appreciate how much it would cost you to live in a city such as New York, so far away from here. I know how much a measure of your love for me your offer is. And we will go, for short visits occasionally, just to make sure my financial interests are being looked after, and to give Janet—and any other children we have—the benefit of knowing both worlds. But I'm not tied to Cordell Enterprises any more, Rebecca. My life is now here with you. It always will be."

She stared at him, not comprehending how that could be so. "But you're chairman."

"Not any longer," he said quietly. "I made up my mind to put someone else in that position before I spoke to Paul."

The shock of his total commitment to her drained the blood from Rebecca's face. "You gave all that up... for me?"

His smile was softly ironic as he lifted a hand to her cheek in a tender caress. "It wasn't so much to give up. The problem was in finding someone to take over from me. Someone who would be good enough. Over the last few months one man proved himself capable of handling everything I threw at him. A guy named Ross Harper. He's probably chairing a board meeting right now, and relishing every moment of it."

Slade called her fearless, but Rebecca had known many moments of intense fear in her life. This one was as paralysing as when she knew Paul's helicopter was going to crash. What Slade had done was just as irreversible, and again it was all because of her. Making a sacrifice of years of leadership and achievement, throwing it away. And if she failed him...

"I wish you hadn't done that, Slade," she said in a strained little voice.

"I wanted to," he assured her. "We're going to have a lifetime marriage, Rebecca. Nothing less would satisfy me, and I know it's what you want, too."

A lifetime marriage... They were her words. If she had given in to him when he had first asked her to marry him, he wouldn't have felt forced to go to such lengths as to sever all his responsibilities to Cordell Enterprises. It was her stubborn independence that had fed Slade's obsessive determination. And he would surely regret what he had done in years to come. How could anyone give up ruling an empire and be satisfied with simply being a husband and father? Eventually he would get bored and feel frustrated and end up hating her.

"You shouldn't have done it. It won't work," she protested, sheer panic squeezing her heart.

"Yes, it will," he answered calmly.

She shook her head in helpless despair. "I wouldn't have given up Wildjanna for you, Slade."

"I know. I knew from the time you faced me over your grandmother's grave that you and Wildjanna were inseparable, Rebecca."

He stroked her cheek with loving tenderness. "Don't be distressed, my darling. I'd been discontented with being chairman of Cordell Enterprises for some time, long before I met you. Then you burst into my life—I was feeling particularly restless and frustrated with everything that day—and you attracted me so much I wanted to pursue the attraction."

His smile held not the slightest twinge of regret. "Best decision I ever made. And when I heard you were carrying my child, I sure as heck knew what I wanted. If I needed any confirmation of my feelings, that first month here with you was more than enough. Apart from which, I really enjoyed working on Wildjanna. It was more solid and real and satisfying than sitting in an office toting up figures and listening to reports. And the stars at night, the clarity of the sky..." He cocked a quizzical eyebrow. "You won't mind if I build an observatory here, will you, Rebecca?"

She shook her head, dazedly hoping she was wrong to worry about their future together.

Slade grinned. "I figured on asking you that *after* we were married. Not that I thought you'd object. I've just been distracted—very happily distracted—by being a new father. In fact, I'm going to give myself a lot of time for such distractions. Astrophysics will be a fine hobby on the side."

Rebecca's inner tension eased a bit more. Slade had always wanted to be an astrophysicist. Maybe he wouldn't miss being the head of Cordell Enterprises after all.

"You know, all the stars we see are only five percent of what's out there," he went on, the eagerness of an enthusiast in his voice. "Scientists call the other ninety-five percent the dark matter. I'm going to work on that dark matter, Rebecca. I'd be happy to spend the rest of my life on that. Just think of all the mysteries of the universe waiting to be uncovered!"

The light of mission in his eyes convinced Rebecca that this was something he really wanted to do.

His focus sharpened on her. "And another thing! We can offer the children who come here for a visit a look at the universe through my telescope. It will round off and complement all that Wildjanna can offer them."

He was right. It would be a marvellous experience.

"You know what else I thought?" Slade continued, his eyes twinkling with the surprise he had in store for her.

Rebecca shook her head again, not trusting herself to speak until all her turbulent emotion had calmed down.

"That day we had to shift the cattle to high ground, it would have saved us a lot of time if we could have tracked them all first by satellite. Once I've got my computers installed in the observatory and hooked in to our satellite, we can always find out where the cattle are, even the most wayward stragglers."

"Our satellite?" Rebecca croaked incredulously.

"Yep. I did tell you Cordell Enterprises financed one, didn't I? The infrared sensor devices are so accurate they can track a moth at a distance of a thousand miles. And I haven't severed all connections with the old firm, Rebecca.

We still hold fifty-one percent of the shares. Who knows? We might have a son who takes after my father. Myself, I reckon I've got more of my grandfather in me.''

Yes, she'd like a son, Rebecca thought dizzily. Slade was still going too fast for her to take everything in. ''Where have you put this satellite?'' she asked.

''Right overhead,'' came the cheerful reply. ''It's in geosynchronous orbit, revolving with us at the same speed as the earth rotates every day. Of course, the sensors are only part of the story. You still need the stock men to round up the cattle and do all the physical chores that have to be done. But there are all sorts of applications to station work we can do on the computer. We can use all the land on Wildjanna and Devil's Elbow much more efficiently, Rebecca. We might even buy out Emilio's if he wants to go back home to Argentina. I reckon we can run the greatest cattle station in the world.''

Rebecca started to laugh as all her worries were comprehensively chased away. Slade was already staking out another empire. A new challenge. With her. And there was no doubt about it now. He was not a city man. He had pioneer blood, too.

He gave her a mock frown. ''Have I said something funny?''

''No.'' She sighed. ''I have this vision of you running a vast cattle station...from your observatory.''

''I don't mind doing the physical work, too,'' he protested.

''Infrared sensors have to be the ultimate in laziness!''

He was smugly unashamed. ''Grandfather Logan would have been proud of me.''

Rebecca laughed, then wound her arms around his neck and kissed him. ''Feel like giving me the benefit of some more brilliant ideas?'' she asked, moving her body against his.

Slade's response was gratifyingly instant. A low sexy growl gravelled from his throat as he swept her off her feet and strode for the bedroom. They passed Milly along the way and the housekeeper asked if anything was wrong.

''No. I've just got this uncontrollable urge to make love to the mother of my child,'' Slade tossed over his shoulder, not pausing in his step.

''Well, at least you're not doing it in front of the horses,'' Milly snapped back at him.

Which convulsed Rebecca with giggles.

Slade paused at their bedroom door. ''That wasn't nice, Milly.''

''Huh!'' the housekeeper scoffed. ''Nothing you could do would shock me any more, Slade Cordell. You get off about your business. I'll keep my eye on the babe.''

''Milly, there's no telling how long this will take,'' Slade lobbed back, then quickly stepped inside the bedroom and closed the door.

It took every second of a full hour for Rebecca to show him how deeply, wildly, passionately, tenderly, totally she loved him. Slade had precisely the same idea. It was such a beautiful time together that when they heard their baby demanding to be fed, Rebecca threw on a gown, hurried to fetch their child from Milly and carried her back to Slade so that they could all be together.

It always fascinated him to watch his daughter latch onto Rebecca's breast and suck so knowingly and greedily. ''Nature sure is a marvellous thing,'' he murmured as the tiny rosebud mouth found its target with unerring instinct once again. ''She's just like you, Rebecca.''

''In what way?'' Rebecca asked, her eyes adoring the big American who had given her everything she had ever dreamed of. Such a big man in every way—mind, heart and soul—the inner him even bigger than the outer him.

Dark blue eyes lovingly caressed her and the baby she held to her breast. "Elemental," he murmured, and heaved a sigh of contentment.

Slade knew he had won more than he had ever dreamed of. Others might look at what he had done and wonder at the losses he had taken in order to have what he had now, but he knew what he had won. This woman who had answered the long questing in his soul…this woman at his side for the rest of his life. And he counted himself a mighty big Texas-size winner—all the way!

AUTHOR'S NOTE

I have, many years ago, given birth to three children. It was at a time when husbands were instantly bustled out of the hospital, and both parents were denied the experience of sharing the birth of their child. I was ignorant of the whole birth process and very much afraid of what I didn't know. Having read so much about it in researching for this story— there is a great deal of literature available now that was not available then—I cannot help feeling cheated of an intimate bond that could have been ours.

I would still be wary of committing myself to a home birth, but hospitals are far more accommodating towards fathers now, and I would urge any prospective parents not to remain ignorant of this miracle of life, but to read, to know, to share and to savour an experience that is uniquely theirs together. I hope I have imparted some of that feeling, which I would have liked so much myself, to you, my readers. To me, it is at the very heart of what loving is all about.

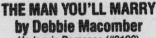

Coming Next Month

Available in June wherever paperback books are sold, or through Harlequin Reader Service:

In the U.S.
P.O. Box 1397
Buffalo, NY
14240-1397

In Canada
P.O. Box 603
Fort Erie, Ontario
L2A 5X3

FREE GIFT OFFER

To receive your free gift, send us the specified number of proofs-of-purchase from any specially marked Free Gift Offer Harlequin or Silhouette book with the Free Gift Certificate properly completed, plus a check or money order (do not send cash) to cover postage and handling payable to Harlequin/Silhouette Free Gift Promotion Offer. We will send you the specified gift.

FREE GIFT CERTIFICATE

ITEM	A. GOLD TONE EARRINGS	B. GOLD TONE BRACELET	C. GOLD TONE NECKLACE
# of proofs-of-purchase required	3	6	9
Postage and Handling	$1.75	$2.25	$2.75
Check one	☐	☐	☐

Name: _____

Address: _____

City: _____ State: _____ Zip Code: _____

Mail this certificate, specified number of proofs-of-purchase and a check or money order for postage and handling to: HARLEQUIN/SILHOUETTE FREE GIFT OFFER 1992, P.O. Box 9057, Buffalo, NY 14269-9057. Requests must be received by July 31, 1992.

PLUS—Every time you submit a completed certificate with the correct number of proofs-of-purchase, you are automatically entered in our MILLION DOLLAR SWEEPSTAKES! No purchase or obligation necessary to enter. See below for alternate means of entry and how to obtain complete sweepstakes rules.

✂ HP2U

ONE PROOF-OF-PURCHASE
To collect your fabulous FREE GIFT you must include the necessary FREE GIFT proofs-of-purchase with a properly completed offer certificate.

(See inside back cover for offer details)

GREAT TEMPTRESSES WORD SEARCH CONTEST

Harlequin wants to give romance readers the chance to receive a fabulous GE SPACEMAKER TV, ABSOLUTELY FREE, just for entering our *Great Temptresses* Word Search Contest. To qualify, complete the word search puzzle below and send it to us so that we receive it by June 26, 1992. Ten entries chosen by random draw will receive a GE SPACEMAKER TV, complete with 6.5" B & W screen, a swivel bracket for easy hanging and built-in AM/FM radio!!!

YOU COULD GET A FREE GE SPACEMAKER TV, JUST FOR PLAYING!

MARILYN MONROE	SALOME
DELILAH	BETTE DAVIS
GRETA GARBO	CLEOPATRA
MADONNA	LAUREN BACALL
MATA HARI	BETTY GRABLE
CHER	SCHEHERAZADE
HELEN OF TROY	MAE WEST
LADY GODIVA	SCARLETT O'HARA

HOW TO ENTER

All the names listed are hidden in the word puzzle grid. You can find them by reading the letters forward, backward, up and down, or diagonally. When you find a word, circle it or put a line through it. Then fill in your name and address in the space provided, put this page in an envelope, and mail it today to:

H1MAY

Harlequin *Great Temptresses* Word Search Contest
Harlequin Reader Service®
P.O. Box 9071
Buffalo, NY 14269-9071

NAME _____

ADDRESS _____

_____

CITY _____ STATE _____ ZIP CODE _____